Fairybridge

For Peter

Fairybridge

Martin Booth

Fairybridge
Martin Booth

Published by Aspect Design 2021.
Malvern, Worcestershire, United Kingdom.

Designed, printed and bound by Aspect Design
89 Newtown Road, Malvern, Worcs. WR14 1PD
United Kingdom
Tel: 01684 561567
E-mail: allan@aspect-design.net
Website: www.aspect-design.net

A copy of this book has been deposited
with the British Library Board

Original cover image by vik173
Cover design by Aspect Design

ISBN 978-1-912078-226-6

*For Beth, who's still
the girl I met on Brownlow Hill*

Preface

I wrote the first three chapters of this novel in the 1990s. It started life as *Carbuncle,* the title Prince Charles bestowed upon the extension to the Tate Gallery in particular and modern architecture in general. An architect myself, I am by nature a modernist, yet for the sake of the story have had to make my protagonist, Michael, a devotee of the Arts and Crafts movement. I do share his admiration of that style but, unlike him, am content to leave it where it belongs in the late nineteenth century.

The embryonic novel had its admirers, including a literary agent who asked to see the rest. There was no rest, of course, so I took early retirement from my local authority job with the intention of writing (almost) full time. A few more chapters ensued. Troubles with the family business, however, took me back to work and when I finally retired again it was to self-build another house in the wilds of Herefordshire. The construction of stone walls and summerhouses supplanted the construction of literary plots, though I did manage the occasional short story, collected and printed in 2018 as *Look Through Any Window.* It took Covid to provide me with the time and motivation to write anything lengthy again.

At the beginning of lockdown, I read through my novel, by then about eight chapters long. It described a world of drawing boards and tee squares, of dyeline printers, office memos and typing pools. No CAD, no mobile phones, messages left on scrap paper to be actioned the following day. I attempted to bring it up to date but failed. I knew little of modern technology, of current legislation, of how a modern drawing office functions. I decided to set my story firmly in the 1990s. The working environment evolves, but human beings, their ambitions and relationships, their strengths and weaknesses, don't change at all. I plunged into writing with a new enthusiasm.

Carbuncle became *An Architect's Dream.* The phrase came from my clerk of works friend, big Al Bishop. An architect's dream is a bricklayer's nightmare, he told me, often. By the time the novel was complete, however, I realised the title was too esoteric. Most people, as pointed out in the book, can only name two architects and care little about their dreams. So *Fairybridge* took the title, Fairybridge Court, around which the narrative revolves, with its Greek Revival portico, looking for all the world like the stately home that, many years ago, I saw burning from the M50. Other than that, the events and characters in this book are fictitious and any resemblance to real persons, living or dead, is purely coincidental.

I would like to thank friends and members of Malvern Writers Circle, past and present, for their help and encouragement; not least those who contributed endorsements for the cover. Mike Thomas read through the novel for me and made some extremely useful suggestions, as did Richard Wall. Then there's George Olson, soon to be, though he doesn't yet know it, my agent in North America.

I would not have been able to devote the time and effort required to finish *Fairybridge* without the patience, skills and understanding of my wife, Beth, and our family. Thank you all.

Chapter One

Michael Maby, Dip. Arch., ARIBA, rang the bell of number two, Princess Margaret Gardens and turned to face the lawn. The signs were not auspicious; a pram half full of water, thistles growing through the exposed innards of an armchair. The gate, installed as part of the Council's refurbishment programme six months previously, and stained a tasteful chestnut brown, had gone, as had the posts which once supported it. In the bedroom of next door someone sang loud and plaintively with the radio, *Would I lie to you, baby, would I lie to you, oh yea!* He rang the bell again.

The woman who eventually answered the door eyed Michael and his survey pad with suspicion. She was greasily dark and of the proportions that Renoir liked to paint. Though it was now mid-morning she was holding together the halves of a diaphanous violet housecoat. Smoke rose from her free hand.

'I'm from the Council,' Michael apologised, showing his identification card, 'I have to check your house to see if any defects have developed since the builders finished. But if it's inconvenient—'

'All the same to me, ducks!' The woman turned sideways in the doorway so that Michael had to squeeze past her into the hall. 'Take me as you find me, though!' Michael had an uneasy feeling that this was an invitation. He took a deep and resolute breath.

The odour which replaced the outside air as the door closed

behind him was at first unidentifiable. There was toast in it and cigarettes but underlying a deeper suffusion of babies and armpits and dogs. Further evidence of the latter manifested itself as dark patches at the junction of skirtings and carpet.

'Still getting rising damp.' The woman intercepted his gaze.

Michael resolved to keep this survey to essentials.

'Any defects you know of?' he asked.

'Them new kitchen cupboards is crap; drawers is allus sticking.'

Michael had carried out much research before specifying those cupboards and had been convinced he was achieving good value for the budget he had been given. He followed the woman stiffly into the kitchen.

There was a marked contrast between this, and the kitchen depicted in the sales brochure. Gone was the string of onions, the pheasant and the carefully scattered herbs. In their place were lager cans, styrene packaging and stacks of egg-smeared plates; so many plates in fact that the classic onyx worktop was hardly visible. One drawer front was missing.

'See, that's what 'appens when you tries to open 'em.'

Michael tried to open one of the other drawers. It was, he had to concede, a little stiff, partly due to the weight of the motorbike battery it contained.

'They move better if you put soft soap on the runners,' he suggested. The woman was aghast.

'I pay my rent,' she said. 'Why should I do it?'

Michael wrote *sticking drawers* in his pad. 'Any other problems?' he asked.

'Them builders ruined my carpet. I'll show you.' She led him by the arm, kicking an empty dog food can out of the way. It clanged against others in the corner.

The living/dining room of number two, Princess Margaret Gardens was dominated by a large open fire, as indeed were all the living/dining rooms of Princess Margaret Gardens. The retention of these features had been at the insistence of the local member, Councillor Marcus Groat, whose estate contained a wood yard. Today, however, the fuel consisted of squared timber, stained chestnut brown. A large section bearing a hinge burned fiercely at the front.

Seated around this fire were two more women and some ten assorted children ranging from junior school age down to babies. The women and the older children wore grubby tee-shirts; the younger wandered naked like grounded cherubim, their faces smeared with snot and butter from the pieces of toast they carried. Discarded nappies lay about the floor.

'Neighbours,' explained the tenant of number two. 'He's from the Council'.

'When you coming to do me?' one of the women asked shrilly.

'He ain't done me yet!' The women cackled.

'Do you want some toast?' the shrill one asked, fishing a slice of bread out of the wrapper in the hearth.

'Thank you, no,' Michael said hastily. 'I'm just looking at the carpet.' The tenant pointed to a small pink plaster stain on the carpet, between a squashed chip and a nappy.

'That was a good carpet before them builders came. Only had it six months!' Michael was going to draw her attention to the strands of the base, clearly visible through wide areas of the pile, but thought better of it.

'I'll mention it to the builder,' he said, making for the door.

In the hall he found the woman had somehow got between him and the front door. She was no longer holding together the front of the violet housecoat.

'Do you want to see upstairs?' she asked. There were more cackles from the living/dining room.

'Oh, I don't think that will be necessary,' he said. 'When you've seen one you've seen them all. No, I'll just have a look out at the back.'

He thought afterwards, if he had not been in a panic, he would have remembered the door he opened served a log-store, might even have noticed its chewed bottom rail. Then he would never have met the Alsatian-wolfhound cross that lived behind it.

* * *

During the period that Michael was trapped in the downstairs toilet of number two, Princess Margaret Gardens, the chief officers of Glostover District Council were holding their weekly working lunch. This began at ten-thirty every Friday in the back room of the Glendower Arms, a venue chosen for its convivial atmosphere and absence of telephones as being conducive to corporate decision making. And the beer was good.

The first two items on the agenda this Friday had been Homelessness (ten minutes) and Chief Officers' Salary Awards. They had gone on, at eleven-forty, to discuss the recent Mutual Appraisal Scheme, whereby staff had exchanged views with middle-management on their relative performances over the past year. Some doubt had been cast on the wisdom of introducing this scheme, following as closely as it did the Assertiveness course for juniors.

At twelve-fifteen they came to Any Other Matters. It was customary at this stage for the chief executive to look questioningly at his officers in an anti-clockwise direction, and equally customary for all to decline. Valuable drinking time was otherwise lost. Today, however, when the raised eyebrows were turned in his direction, the treasurer shifted uncomfortably and cleared his throat.

'I'm afraid,' he said, 'that I have a discrepancy to report.' There were groans around the table. Discrepancies in the Treasury meant cuts in the Capital Programme and, God knows, they had had their fair share of those in recent years!

But 'No,' said the treasurer, 'this error's on the credit side. We've got more than we thought we had this year.' Interest showed itself on the faces of those chief officers whose departments spent money. The director of Housing leaned forward.

'What are we talking in, George? Hundreds? Thousands?'

'Well, it's, er, millions, actually,' said the treasurer. 'Five million! And fifty-two!' There was a long silence. Then the chief planner spoke slowly.

'Let me get this straight, George. In your little piggy bank you have five million pounds that you didn't know was there?'

The treasurer nodded unhappily. 'It was the computer programme we bought from Strathgorbal Council, on the cheap if you remember, to deal with the rates, when Finance Committee wouldn't buy a proper one. It seems that there was an in-built assumption of fifty per cent non-payment. And practically the whole of our honest citizens coughed up, didn't they?' He slumped disconsolately in his chair.

'I suppose,' said the solicitor eventually, 'that we can't just give it back.' The others glared at him. The Legal Department's budget was confined largely to pink ribbon and paper clips.

'It's not as simple as that.' The treasurer explained that the Ministry was intending to tailor spending approvals to the reserves held by individual councils. Reward for Thrift it was called. The Government had discovered a correlation between councils with large reserves and marginal seats and an election was looming.

'So, if we give the money back, we'll lose the spending approval too. We need to keep it for a few months and then spend it before they change the rules again. Any ideas, gentlemen?'

* * *

The twelve houses which constituted Princess Margaret Gardens had been built in 1946 to accommodate returning soldiers, thanks to the generosity of Marcus Groat's father, the late Henry Groat, also a councillor, who had donated a field to the Rural District, the year before becoming its chairman. The field was half a mile outside the village of Drabley and well suited, he felt, for social housing, being sheltered by a belt of dense woodland from the prevailing weather and the windows of Groat Hall. It was, unfortunately, directly across a small valley from the country seat of the Groat's hereditary enemy, Lord Drabley, who, nevertheless, had felt unable to object, following his 'Homes for Heroes' speech in the Upper House earlier that year.

The houses were of the design referred to by local architect, Frank Wright FRIBA, as type 5D; that is to say, they had three bedrooms, were semi-detached and Tyrolean rendered from the head of the ground floor steel windows to the eaves. To avoid expensive roadworks, they had been built close against the lane, creating back gardens capable of supporting a small milk cow, had the returning soldiers been so inclined.

The size of the gardens had certainly persuaded some of their successors to exercise their right to buy. Looking back down the lane from number twelve, Michael could identify these houses by their colonial doors, their UPVC Tudor windows and strikingly coloured rendering. Their converted gas street lamps stood out like beacons amid the gardens of the Council's recent improvements, now reverting to a state of equilibrium with nature. Outside number twelve, the last of his inspections, a wheel-less Ford Consul, its battered body supported on concrete blocks, dripped sump oil slowly onto the herringbone brick pavers of the new parking bay; a withered sapling drooped like a camp comedian's wrist.

Michael wondered, not for the first time, if it had been a good career move coming to Glostover. His own car, he was relieved to see, still retained its wheels. He tossed the survey pad into the back seat and set off gloomily for the office. It had not been a good day so far and a return to his desk was unlikely to improve it. Out of sight of Princess Margaret Gardens, however, the sun came out and there were trees with birds singing in them. The lane plunged into a froth of apple orchards.

It was country like this which had drawn Michael from a promising job in the West Midlands. The move had been romantically inspired rather than rational. Like many Brummies before him, he was entranced by the Marches, by their deep rivers and long escarpments, their English softness on the hard edge of Wales. Glostover was a convenience, a temporary arrangement, he had partly convinced a doubting Andrea, just to get us down there, until something better turns up. But then there was the Miners' Strikes, the drop in commercial confidence, and the suspension of recruitment.

Their house too was a stopgap, soulless and affordable on a

bland estate, to give them time to find exactly the right place. But the mortgage rate had changed, and the house was no longer affordable. Soulless it remained.

The likelihood of finding a place which was exactly right for both of them was, in truth, small. Andrea's place looked vaguely Elizabethan but had two modern bathrooms, a fully equipped kitchen and was within walking distance of the shops. Despite five years of marriage to an architect she remained resolutely suburban. Michael's house, on the other hand, was miles from the shops and built by one of his wealthier fellow émigrés from Birmingham on a south facing slope at the turn of the century. It was designed by Charles Voysey, William Lethaby or ideally, and here Michael approached veneration, by the great C. P. Hopwood.

How the move from semi-detached to stately living was to be achieved was as undefined in Michael's head as the Tudor style was in Andrea's. It involved a drawing office in the library, self-sufficiency and conversion of the stable block to holiday lets. Michael strode through the gardens of this dream in green wellingtons, a springer spaniel at his heel and a golden-haired child on his shoulders. Both were perfectly behaved.

His reverie came abruptly to an end as the lane hit the Glostwich by-pass, the girdle of tarmac which for the present at least restricted the spread of urban development into the countryside. He looked at his watch. It was four-fifteen. A left turn to the office would mean dealing with the inevitable notes on his desk:

> Urgent; window sticking at Morton Court. Please ring Orifice Plumbing Products re missed appointment with their rep.

He turned right. He felt in need of the comfort his wife could dispense.

* * *

In the Glendower Arms the working lunch continued animatedly through the afternoon, fuelled by chicken chasseur and Banks's Best Bitter. Visions of large capital projects floated almost visibly over the chief officers' heads. It had been some time since anything larger than a public toilet had been built in Glostover and each chief officer had his own ideas for disposing of the multi-million-pound windfall.

The leisure manager wanted a Sports Complex. The director of Housing wanted two Old Peoples' Homes but on being reminded by the treasurer that revenue income could not be used for housing confined himself to opposing sports facilities.

'What this district really needs,' said the chief planner, 'is a business park. Bring in the jobs and the houses will follow.'

'That's all very well,' the director of Services argued, 'but how do you think my sewage treatment works are going to cope with the increased load? Not to mention refuse collection. I need a complete new fleet.'

The chief executive listened to the acrimony with growing alarm.

The severe shortage of funds which had existed since his appointment the previous year had induced a camaraderie among his lieutenants, a sort of Dunkirk spirit. This windfall indicated change, a wind which threatened to rattle the fence on which he liked to sit. His secretary, when asked by a puzzled councillor what made the chief executive tick, had thought for a moment and replied, 'Compromise; he's very strong on that!'

The chief executive scanned the options for a compromise that would appeal to all the group. He found one. In the 1974 Local Government Reorganisation, Glostover District Council had been created from the bits that surrounding councils had rejected. As a result, it had no natural centre, and the available offices were scattered around the constituent towns in widely disparate and largely unsuitable buildings. These ranged from a Victorian Gothic hotel with flat roofed extensions, the Planning Department, to the converted glue factory which Housing shared with Environmental Health. Travel between these buildings for the frequent corporate meetings which took place was inconvenient and one, though admittedly not the main, reason why the chief officers were assembled in the Glendower.

The chief executive beamed myopically round the table.

'Gentlemen,' he said, 'what would you say to a brand-new purpose-built civic centre?'

* * *

It was apparent to Michael as soon as he opened the front door that comfort would be in short supply that evening. Andrea, emerging from the kitchen, was still in uniform; the lemon and grey of Cloisters, the private clinic where she worked as a physiotherapist. Her frown and the large knife she gripped in a surgical glove suggested that Michael had disturbed her in some ghastly operation.

'You didn't get the message,' she accused.

'What message was that, pet?' he countered lamely.

'Cheese; I needed cheese!'

Michael explained that he had not been back to the office, that it had been a bad day. He told her about the Alsatian-wolfhound cross but not the violet housecoat. Andrea sighed, managing to imply dereliction of duty and cowardice in one gesture. Her day had been hell, she did not have to say, but was she complaining?

'Well, you'll just have to have your cauliflower cheese without the cheese, that's all,' she said, flouncing back into the kitchen. Michael picked up his mail from the hall table. If truth were told he preferred his cauliflower cheese without the cauliflower too.

'And I suppose that's one of your picture books.'

Michael discarded the bills and turned over the brown cardboard wrapped package beneath them. Yes, that would be 'Hopwood, the Middle Years,' a lavishly illustrated volume he had ordered some weeks previously from the RIBA bookshop. He decided, despite himself, to open it when Andrea had gone to bed, and he could cut the price off the corner of the dustsheet.

'Just a sale bargain, pet; they're giving them away just now.'

Once it was on the shelves, she would never notice it. The only time that Andrea took books off the shelves was to dust them. He wandered into the kitchen and opened the fridge. There was a fair-sized lump of Cheddar where he remembered it being, in the smoked plastic box marked *butter* inside the door.

'How am I expected to find it if you put it in there?' Andrea said.

Michael disguised a smile. He slid his arms round her waist as she dismembered vegetables at the sink and kissed the back of her neck. Her hair moved like ripe barley under his breath. He recalled how its pale gold had first attracted him; that and the cornflower blue of her eyes. Later he had come to realise that blue was the colour of distance.

They had met as students; he at School of Architecture, she at the Nurses Training College which providence had built on the same campus. For three years the juxtaposition had fed an ever-changing round of parties and of pairings and when the music stopped Michael and Andrea had found themselves together.

It was during the time they lived together on a grant and a student nurse's wage that Michael had developed his dislike of cauliflower cheese.

Nor was it Andrea's favourite meal. She believed, however, that for Michael it was a symbol of the simplicity of their early marriage and so continued to serve it. What she hankered for was the French cuisine, the rich pates and expensive wines which, she imagined, were the regular diet of the clinic's clientele. She saw the limousines in which they arrived, the exclusive labels on the clothes they carelessly threw over chairs, the opulence of their lingerie. Some days, and today was one of them, their assumed aches and pains made her feel like tipping them abruptly from the treatment couch. She was envious too of the consultants who relieved them of their moles and their money and drove away in BMWs. Why did Michael not have a job like that?

Maybe she should have gone for a doctor. She could have had Oliver, who had once fondled her left breast at a party and was now married to her friend. Andrea was reminded of the letter which had arrived with the bills and Michael's book. She removed Michael's hand as she had once removed Oliver's.

'Jane wrote,' she said, scraping the now thoroughly humiliated cauliflower into a saucepan. 'She and Oliver are coming for a weekend. They fancy a change of scene and we haven't seen them for a while.'

'That'll be nice,' Michael said. He was only half lying. He had once partnered Jane at tennis and still remembered her rear view at the net. The thought of a weekend of Oliver, however, filled him with gloom. It meant comparisons; how well Oliver was doing, what car Oliver was driving, where Oliver was about to attend an international conference. On occasions like this Michael usually took refuge in social commitment. It would be difficult, he realised, to be convincingly committed to Princess Margaret Gardens.

'Oliver's just been offered a partnership,' said Andrea.

Chapter Two

The sky was threatening when Michael reached the office the following day. He was not surprised, therefore, to find Arthur Brickbatt sitting on his desk drinking coffee. When it was about to rain cows lay down on the tops of hills and clerks of works came into the office. Arthur was reading the messages which had been stuck to Michael's drawing board. At Michael's approach he scrambled to mock attention, the exertion causing his potbelly to burst two buttons off the front of his checked shirt.

'Begging your pardon, sir; and how was the cauliflower cheese?' he said. Michael gave him what he hoped was a stern look.

'Fine,' he said coldly. He would, he thought, have to have a word with Andrea about these domestic messages. If the Council would provide its outside workers with those mobile phones, it would be so much easier. He put his briefcase in the space vacated by Arthur's bottom and read the other notes on his board.

Urgent; Pleases ring warden, Morton Lodge. Carpet tiles lifting; fatal accidents imminent, and Mr Slymer of Orifice Products sorry to hear of your illness, will contact you again when you are fully recovered.

'I told him you had gastroenteritis,' Ronnie Barge said glumly from the adjacent desk, 'it sounded better than just swanning around the countryside!'

'I was doing the defects survey at Princess Margaret Gardens,' Michael protested, 'I just got tied up for a while at number two.' He regretted the phraseology as he spoke.

'Bondage, eh?' Arthur Brickbatt smirked. 'You little devil! And there's me thinking you was an 'appily married man, grocery shopping and that.' He winked at Ronnie as Michael reddened. 'I remember her at number two. Them builders was in and out of that house all day. Wonder they ever finished the contract. Do you know,' he lowered his voice conspiratorially, 'there was a plasterer's labourer who got in there who's never been seen since. Nice young lad he was too.'

Michael took out his set square and drawing instruments and uncovered the partly finished drawing on his board, the plan and elevations of a washhouse for the gypsy site he was designing. It was, he felt, a little gem, with its lancet window in the gable, its finials at the ridge; almost Cottage Ornée in style. He toyed with the idea of having the bargeboards carved to suggest the traditional Romany caravan. But what the Gypsy Solution Sub-Committee wanted, he knew, were functional features; metered water, washable floors and concealed ducts to protect the copper pipework from premature recycling.

He leaned over to check a dimension on the site plan, already completed and laid out next to his desk. Individual caravan pitches were grouped around a central manoeuvring space. They were surrounded in turn by a belt of thick planting, the whole enclosed by a two-metre-high stock proof fence. The official line was that this was to protect the camp from encroachment by farm animals. The reverse was in fact true.

One corner of the site labelled *play space* was indicated as grass by meticulous dotting. In the centre of this was a large coffee ring, still wet. The tracing paper was beginning to cockle. Michael stared at it in dismay.

'Look what you've done, you prat!' he shouted at Brickbatt who had now finished his coffee and was in the process of adjusting the contents of his voluminous trousers. This was a ritual preparation for going out on site, a sort of girding of loins for the fray. The clerk of works peered at the drawing.

'Sorry, mate,' he said, contrite for a moment, then more cheerfully, 'couldn't you turn it into a tree?'

'Or a hedgehog roasting pit?' suggested Ronnie Barge.

It was perhaps fortunate that the principal architect chose this moment to put his head round the door.

'Could I have a word with you in my office, Mr Maby,' he said.

* * *

Michael had never felt at ease in Maxwell Spynk's office. It was a high-ceilinged room in the originally Victorian hotel which formed the nucleus of the department. The white travertine marble fireplace with grapes and cherubs remained, the one vestige of opulence in the room. The carpet was mid-grey, the chairs, on one of which Michael now sat, were upholstered in grey tweed. A bookcase and the conference table between he and the principal architect were black ash on chromed tubular steel, the walls and paintwork white, not white with a subtle hint of anything, just white. Mounted on them were photographs of glass and steel buildings. The photographs were monochrome too. A grey-green succulent plant, non-flowering, stood sculpturally in the bay window.

Maxwell Spynk squared up the papers in front of him. He was a thin ascetic man in his mid-fifties with a thin disembodied voice. A yellow tie was the one concession to colour in his dress. Sometimes he wore a red one.

'Well, er . . .' he checked his notes, 'Michael; you've been with us for almost three years now. The work you've done on modernisations and public conveniences and, er . . .'

Michael prompted him, 'Gypsy sites.'

'Has been, er, most satisfactory. Er, most satisfactory.'

He had a disconcerting habit of addressing his speech to an angel floating somewhere beyond the right shoulder of the person in front of him. Communication appeared to pain him.

'So, the time has come to give you more responsibility. The chief and I would like you to undertake a feasibility study for, and I must emphasise at this stage that this is strictly confidential, a new civic centre for the district of Glostover. What do you say?'

Michael said 'Great.' It was inadequate to express his delight. At last, a project he could get his teeth into, something that would justify the years of training, actual architecture. 'Do we have a brief, Mr Spynk, or a site?'

The principal architect smiled thinly. *A Brief!* He remembered those college schemes where the theoretical client knew exactly what he wanted from his building; a restaurant serving seventy-two meals in two sittings, storage for five thousand boxes, each measuring four by three by—! Briefs in Glostover were something you wore for a day and put in the wash.

'I think we can say you have a free hand at the moment, Michael. Except that the building must accommodate all departments and a new Council Chamber. As for a site, the planners have something in mind. They're expecting you this

morning. It's important that we move quickly while the money's
available.'

He closed the file, thus indicating that the interview was at
an end. Michael rose to leave, his mind buzzing.

'And remember,' the principal architect said to the angel as
Michael opened the door, 'this is strictly confidential!'

'So, what's all this about new offices?' Ronnie Barge asked.

Michael had barely reached his desk. Flummoxed for a moment
he stopped and stared at his colleague, perched atop a fully
extended draughtsman's chair like a glum gnome on a toadstool.
His squatness may have contributed to the number of times he
had been overlooked in favour of younger men. Michael had just
become the latest of these.

Ronnie compensated for this lack of recognition by his
employers by extracting all he could from them. He claimed
every tenth of a mile he drove on office business, and ensured he
was on site at the strategic times for qualifying for lunch, tea and
even breakfast allowance. His drawers were full of replacement
drawing pens, of staples, paper clips and manila envelopes. He
would arrive some mornings in great discomfort so as to use the
office toilet rather than his own.

Ronnie Barge lived for the day when he could take early
retirement on maximum pension. The exact date was written on
his heart. The day after that he was going overland to Sri Lanka.
He had not quite got around to it in the Sixties.

Despite appearances, however, Ronnie Barge was the best
informed erk in the district council, the stock of its grapevine.
For years he had been the department's union rep, not from
any socialist commitment, but because the position gave him
immediate access to all committee minutes and agendas. He had

a network of informants. It was said he knew the chief executive's mind before the chief executive had up made it. The *Glostwich Bugle* consulted him.

'I hear they're going to be at Fairybridge Court,' he said.

Michael smiled in a knowing way. He put his jacket on. This time Ronnie had to be wrong. Fairybridge Court was a ruin three miles outside the town in open countryside. The draft Structure Plan had zoned its grounds as an Area of Outstanding Natural Beauty, suitable only for limited recreational use such as a picnicking spot or bird sanctuary.

'I'm not allowed to say at present,' he said, slipping a notepad and a couple of pens into his jacket pocket. 'If anyone rings, I'm over with the planners.'

* * *

'Well, there it is,' said Geoff Lomax, the central area planning officer, 'or rather, there it was!' They were standing between his car and Michael's on an unmade track surrounded by birch wood. The track had left the road half a mile back. In front of them was a vast area of brick and concrete rubble, punctuated by charred exclamation marks of blackened timber. Ferns grew amongst it, and here and there an adventurous birch had taken root.

'Fairybridge Court in all its glory! Built by the Fairybridge family at the beginning of the nineteenth century. Greek Revival, double height portico. Restored in the 1890s and demolished by one G. I. Schultze in 1944.'

Michael looked at him quizzically.

'The family's fortune declined somewhat in the thirties. Sir Penn Fairybridge must have been over the moon when the Yanks took it over during the war. Thought the compensation would solve all his problems. They stored ammunition here, which was all very well until G. I. Schultze had too much of the local brew and went hunting pheasants with a flame thrower. Good thinking really, shot and roasted in one operation! Anyway, that was the end of the court, and Schultze. I believe he was posthumously court-martialled for it.'

'Are there any records of the building?' Michael asked.

'We haven't any but the County Archivist may have something. I don't think it was anything special; the Fairybridges used a Birmingham architect for the restoration. Didn't hold with London airs and graces. Gosplett, he was called, William Gosplett, or was it Henry? Ever come across his work?'

Michael confessed he had not. A greater spotted woodpecker swooped across the clearing and landed on a dead birch not twenty yards from where they were standing. They watched it probing the rotten wood with its road-drill of a beak.

Michael said, 'Should we really be building a civic centre here?'

Geoff Lomax grinned.

'That depends on whether you're asking me as a planner or a pragmatist. As a planner I would say over my dead body. As I prefer to live and prosper, however, I could be persuaded it was a replacement for an existing building; especially if it incorporated some recreational use. Anyway, form your own opinion. I have to go and explain to an irate gentleman why he can't tack a conservatory onto his barn conversion.'

He wound his window down before driving off.

'By the way, you know who owns this place now, don't you? Marcus Groat, chairman of the Council? Evidently his wife is a distant cousin of the Fairybridges. But don't let that influence your thinking!'

After he had gone Michael clambered into the wreckage of the court. The rubble was thicker than he had at first perceived, for the house had collapsed into its own basement. Black holes gaped between the chunks of masonry, making each step hazardous. The presence of a basement would make the foundations expensive, unless he could utilise it in some way, parking perhaps. Yes, why not hide all the cars underneath the building. This environmentally friendly idea made him feel more positive. Maybe the site should be redeveloped; it was a god-awful mess at present.

At what had been the front of the house, facing south, the ground fell away to a choked-up lake. Beyond it the panorama was magnificent. Where the lawns must have been were several cedars, mostly blasted, and the remains of a watercourse. He followed it down to the lake.

It was not until he came up against tall reeds and his feet began to sink into mud that he turned to look at the site. He wanted to capture its essence, to fix an impression in his mind for future hours at the drawing board; to see, if the Muse was with him, the shape of a new building on the skyline, rising, as it were, from the ashes. He was quite surprised, therefore, to see a building already on the skyline.

It was on a knoll, to the left of the ruin he had crossed and separated from it by a small coppice, which was why he had previously been unaware of its presence. In shape and size, it resembled a barn, but all detail was lost in a dense covering of ivy. As he climbed back towards it, however, an open porch became discernible, halfway down the long side. It was supported on stone columns with a curious lattice-like decoration. Stooping into it under the ivy he discovered a round-arched doorway to the main building.

His entry caused dozens of jackdaws to rise cackling into the air. There was nothing to stop them for the roof had long gone. Huge baulks of timber from it lay on the floor like some giant's abandoned game of spillikins. The walls, including the gables, were improbably intact.

Michael picked his way through the debris. The remains of campfires, bottles and several condoms betrayed the building's present use. From messages on the walls, he learned that Tracy B. was a slag and that unusual services could be supplied by a certain Tarquin. The characters *C.P.H. 1896* were carved in more elegant style on one of the fallen beams.

High up on the east gable the impression of a cross showed faintly on a patch of tenacious plaster, on the opposite gable a round aperture. Michael was gazing at this when the first drops of rain portended by Arthur Brickbatt began to fall through the missing roof. By the time he reached the car he was soaked.

Chapter Three

'So, you're still with the Council,' Oliver said.

Michael put down his pint, drained of just its top two inches. He had hoped for a longer respite from Oliver's first assault.

'For the moment,' he hedged, aware that he always added *for the moment* when admitting where he worked. 'Until the job scene improves.'

They were sitting in the lounge bar of the Jolly Huntsman, popular for its real ale and false beams and its proximity by foot to Michael's housing estate. Despite this advantage, however, they had come in Oliver's new silver green Corvette Coupé, achieving sixty miles per hour on the straight bit of Falklands Drive. Something to do with torque, Oliver explained.

They had left the ladies, as Oliver liked to call them, at home; the custom in this relationship being that Friday night was for the men. It was joked that this left the ladies free to compare notes about them, a prospect which, Michael observed, perturbed his companion less than himself. Michael would, in any case, have preferred mixed company. Having a drink with Oliver was like being trapped in a lift with an evangelist, except that Oliver's creed was capitalism. In his wallet he carried an icon of the Iron Lady and a text which claimed that the tough would inherit the earth. A public sector worker presented a soul for redemption.

'Ever thought of going out on your own?' he asked.

Michael drained another few inches from his glass. Here it
came, the attempted conversion.

'Of course,' he said, 'but I'm not that interested in bathroom
extensions. At least where I am, I get some interesting jobs to
do.' He told Oliver about the civic centre. At the time of their
last weekend together he had been specifying kitchen units for
Princess Margaret Gardens. His self-justification this time was
more convincing. Oliver, however, was not impressed.

'So, you'll be getting a rise for this? I thought not,' he scoffed,
reading Michael's face. 'Just think of the fees you'd be earning
on this Centre if you were in private practice.'

'But I wouldn't land that sort of job if I was in practice,'
Michael insisted.

'Come on, Michael. It just a question of knowing the right
people. Play squash, join the golf club.' He threw an arm around
Michael's shoulders. 'Listen: you know how fond I am of you and
Andrea. Why don't I get you an intro to—' and here he glanced
around the room, 'the Brotherhood.'

'What do you mean, the Brotherhood?' Michael asked. Oliver
withdrew his arm as if stung.

'Keep your voice down, old chap. Never know who's listening.'
He winked, first with his right eye, then with his left. 'You know,
the Ancient Order!'

Michael still looked blank.

'The Pargetters!' Oliver hissed. He looked sharply at the
barman who was studiously polishing lipstick off a glass at the
far end of the bar.

'Oh them!' Michael said. 'I didn't know you were one of that
lot. Don't you dress up and deflower virgins and things.' Oliver
laughed nervously.

'There are certain ceremonies. What it's really about, however, is maintaining standards, raising funds for charity, that sort of thing.' He plumped himself up on the barstool like a parrot that had been observed falling off its perch. 'And you have to believe in God, of course.'

'I don't think it's my scene,' Michael said. 'But thanks for the thought.'

'Your choice, naturally, old chap. Offer still stands if you change your mind.'

For a moment the atmosphere was cooler than the beer, though this was not unusual in the Jolly Huntsman.

'So, you're still driving the old jalopy,' Oliver said.

* * *

In rooms above a High Street estate agent, the local kiln of the Ancient Order of Pargetters was meeting that very night, as it did on the first Friday of every new moon. Formal proceedings had been completed and the assembly had moved from the Inner Sanctum to the bar.

Journeyman Jenkins, known elsewhere as the chief executive of Glostover District Council, looked around at the sumptuously robed elders, the apprentices in their smocks, and felt a deep sense of history: a history that stretched back to the Middle Ages, to the time when the guild had been granted a charter by Edward the Second and their golden-haired apprentice, Will Smudge, was appointed a royal page. Since then, the Ancient Order had been a stalwart defender of the monarchy, more specifically the Protestant monarchy. Under the later Stuarts it had been forced underground, literally so. The reference to local branches as *kilns* was a relic of the days when meetings had been held in the cave-like ovens where lime was burnt for pargetting.

Secrecy stemmed from those days too; it survived in the coded greetings to strangers, like the one Jenkins had received at his interview for the chief executive's post: 'Was thy journey long?' And its response, 'Yea, but the sights thereon were wondrous!'

Across the room he could see the councillor who had so addressed him, resplendent in the crimson robe of grand chancellor. Journeyman Jenkins approached him deferentially, his right hand holding the lobe of his left ear in the prescribed manner. He saw the grand chancellor's small eyes turn towards him.

'Ah, Hywel!' The acknowledgement simultaneously dismissed the group which was fawning around him. 'Have a drink; straight Scotch, isn't it?'

Jenkins accepted, gratified that the grand chancellor remembered, though in truth he took his whisky liberally diluted with soda. He perched on the edge of the seat proffered and watched the grand chancellor mould himself into the armchair opposite. Standing, the robes of office had a dignifying effect on his ample figure, seated less so. Their crimson clashed with his complexion. Marcus Groat had inherited both the Groats' tendency to ginger colouring and the flat snout-like features of his mother's line. The combination was unfortunate. There were some who claimed to detect in his presence a faint smell of pork; those, admittedly, who had reason to begrudge his success. Jenkins, nevertheless, found himself sniffing.

'And how are things proceeding, Hywel?'

The small eyes perused his face. Jenkins took out a handkerchief and dabbed at his nose.

'Well, Marcus, well. A report will be going to Policy and Finance Committee next week. I have the draft for you here,' He pushed a thick sheaf of pink paper across the table. Groat ignored it.

'What does it say when you cut the crap?'

Jenkins had worked until after midnight for three days to embellish the meagre case for centralised offices. He was rather put out to hear his artistry so described. With dignity, however, he summarised the argument: the cost efficiency of a single building, the *one-stop shop* for the public, the capital to be gained from selling the present offices.

'I hope you're not promising rates cuts.' Groat said.

'I think the phrase used is *reducing the likelihood of further increases*.' Jenkins knew his ratepayers needed to perceive the possibility of financial gain if the project was to go ahead. Civic pride was not widespread in Glostover. There were even some councillors who would need convincing. With each agenda, except the one for the *Bugle*, he would be enclosing a letter describing a prestigious Council Chamber and pointing out that a council with an efficient new headquarters would be well placed to become the single-tier authority the Government was threatening to impose on the area, thus, diluting opposition strongholds. The letter would also hint that less staff were required to run such a building.

'I take it, Hywel, that the staff are not aware of that point?'

'Good Lord, no. Staff consultation will begin once the decision's made.'

Marcus Groat sipped his whisky thoughtfully, his small eyes focused on the great project ahead.

'And the site, Hywel, what of the site?'

'A shortlist of five sites has been drawn up for Planning Committee. Three are non-starters. Fairybridge Court will be played down. The planning officer will overstate the case for the town centre site, emphasising its advantages for the underprivileged. This will naturally antagonise the majority party, who will be inclined in any case to the cheaper price you have so generously set on Fairybridge Court.'

'You seem very confident, Hywel.' Groat's eyes were marbles.

Jenkins quailed inwardly. Despite the homework he had done one could never be sure how local politicians would vote, particularly the independents who swung between liberality and fascism. His mouth formed a smile

'The architects are already preparing a sketch design for the site. Spynk tells me it's progressing well. There is, of course, the delicate matter of your position as chairman to consider.' The grand chancellor grunted.

'Taken care of, Hywel, taken care of. I will be away on business on the day of Finance and Resources Committee. My deputy, Councillor Macready, will take the chair. Won't you, Angus?' he said to the wiry man in a royal blue robe who had just approached holding his ear.

'If,' he added, 'he hasn't gone down with flu or something. Everyone seems to be sniffing tonight. Ought to take more care of yourselves, like I do.'

* * *

The sketch scheme was not, in fact, progressing well. Every night for a week the cleaner had found Michael's bin full of screwed-up balls of tracing paper. Had she been curious the cleaner would have discovered on that paper strange hieroglyphics; rough circles and squares labelled *foyer, cncl chmbr,* and *comp suite,* with broken lines running between them and arrows of many hues. She may have recognized the triangular sketches which interspersed them as roof shapes. She would certainly have understood the six-inch-high letters, *S H I* and *T,* scrawled across the lot in red marker pen.

The cleaner, however, had no time to be curious. She had merely emptied the whole crackling mass, with Michael's banana skin and Ronnie Barge's half-eaten corned beef sandwiches, into her sack and gone about her business muttering. How was she supposed to do her floor in the allotted thirty-six point five minutes if people left the place in this state? She polished what she could see around the drawings.

The trouble was, as Michael had complained to Ronnie Barge, there were no design limitations on Fairybridge Court. It was a green field site. On most sites the presence of other buildings dictated the number of storeys, the orientation, even, perhaps, the style. At Fairybridge Court there was nothing, except a ruin. The sky was the limit, and the sky was empty.

Michael was lacking a theme. He had been searching for one all week. It had been on his mind during the weekend. It was the reason for his curtness with Oliver in the Jolly Huntsman, for the air of distance which had caused Jane to ask Andrea if all was well and which Andrea put down to sulking following her headache on Thursday night.

Even now on Sunday morning as the four of them walked the ridge above the town, Michael was not fully occupied with the view. This was partly due to the large quantity of wine he had consumed the previous evening. Oliver had impressed Andrea by correctly identifying this at first tasting as Bergerac; not so Michael who had spotted him earlier examining the bottle as it breathed in the other room. After dinner they had played bridge which Michael and Jane had lost heavily as a result of his inability to remember which cards had been played. A further game of Trivial Pursuits was abandoned, with Michael ahead, when Oliver accidentally upset the board. He had just claimed Steven Spielberg as the director of *Psycho*. After that they just drank.

The Bells of Saint Bronwen's were ringing in the town below. The sound wafted up to them like waves of nausea. Michael wanted to be alone. The Bergerac, however, did not appear to have affected Oliver.

'Just the place,' he was enthusing, 'plenty of uplift, few trees! You could travel miles from here.'

Oliver's latest hobby was paragliding. In previous years he had taken up windsurfing, mountain biking and clay pigeon shooting, in addition to the golf. Whenever there was a new sport, Oliver adopted it. He bought all the equipment, top of the range, joined the Association, read the magazine. The next year he would equally quickly go off the sport, having failed to star, sell the equipment for a fraction of what he paid for it and take up a new craze.

'Why don't you do something like paragliding?' Andrea said. 'Get your head out of all those books! Oliver's always doing something exciting.'

Michael hoped that the next craze would be alligator wrestling, preferably in the nude. He knelt to tie his bootlace, allowing the others to get ahead. The breeze on his skin felt good. He let it wash over him, face turned to the clouds it herded in from Wales. On a rock close by, a sparrow-sized bird dipped to its own call, the sort of bird he normally ignored. Today he noticed its soft grey and apricot, the black highwayman's mask it was wearing.

'It's a wheatear, isn't it?'

The quiet voice behind him was enough to send the bird flitting away over the bracken, a flash of white at its tail. He turned to see Jane watching its flight.

'I don't honestly know,' he said. They only had pigeons where I come from. And starlings,' he recalled.

They started after the others, now fifty yards ahead. Oliver was describing something with extravagant movements of the arms. Andrea's laughter came back to them on the breeze.

'I didn't know you were interested in wildlife,' Michael said.

'Dad used to take me birdwatching. Now it gives me something to do while Oliver's paragliding. He thinks the binoculars are for watching him.' They laughed.

'You seem very serious this weekend,' Jane said. 'I asked Andrea if something was wrong.' She did not tell him what Andrea had said.

Michael explained about the civic centre, hesitantly at first in case of boring her, more enthusiastically as she listened. Voicing the problems seemed to make them less insoluble. His head began to clear. As they came off the ridge into the trees, Jane asked,

'Who was the architect you were always so keen on? Hopwood, wasn't it? What would he have done? How would he have designed a civic centre?'

Michael glanced at the pretty face beside him. He was impressed. Most people could only name two architects and C. P. Hopwood would not have been one of them. Out of the wind her perfume was discernible. He could not identify that either, but he liked it.

Jane and Oliver departed after tea. They left behind them a quietness which was partly anti-climax, partly relief. The empty

bottles and disorder which had been the stuff of weekend were
now an irritation. Michael cleared and vacuumed the ground floor
while Andrea washed up. If they had had a dishwasher, Andrea
said, there would have been more time to enjoy themselves. They
watched a programme about dolphins they had seen before, then
Michael put on a record. Chopin, for relaxing, he said. Andrea fell
asleep. At ten o'clock her headache returned, and she went to bed.

Despite the Chopin Michael was still restless. Tomorrow
was Monday and another uninspired day at the drawing board.
He made himself an Ovaltine. What would Hopwood have
done? He took *The Middle Years* from the bookshelf where it
had remained since he had hidden it from Andrea and began
reverently to turn the glossy pages. There they were, the estate
workers cottages, the church halls on which Hopwood had first
practised his art, the style which came to fruition in his great
country houses already evident.

Michael had only reached page nineteen when a photograph
caught his eye. It was a stone capitol carved with the grotesque
heads of mythical beasts, illustrating, the text claimed, Hopwood's
mastery of Norse detailing. The column itself was decorated with
a lattice pattern. Michael upset his Ovaltine.

Surely not! He went for a cloth to the kitchen. It was then that
he remembered the initials on the beam in the ruined chapel:
C. P. H. 1894. The revelation sank through his mind like milk
through carpet. Was it possible that the chapel, the chapel on his
site, was an early Hopwood? On impulse he turned to the index
in the back of the book. *Glass, Gloucestershire, Gosplett.* Page
forty-two. And there he found his evidence, albeit circumstantial.
It was encapsulated in just three sentences!

Between October 1893 and March 1895 Hopwood was employed by the Birmingham architect, Henry Gosplett. The association was not a happy one as Gosplett was a classicist and disapproved of Hopwood's eclectic tendencies. No examples of Hopwood's work from this period survive.

Michael was inclined to think otherwise!

Chapter Four

Once the idea had come to him of using the chapel as a council chamber, Michael explained to Maxwell Spynk, the rest of the scheme had fallen into place. They were talking over the drawings laid out on the principal architect's desk, which showed the chapel restored and connected by a bridge over the end of an extended lake to the first floor of an office block where the court itself had once stood. The drawings were freehand, in fibre-tip and had a conviction missing from earlier attempts.

'You're sure the chapel, if that's what it is, merits restoration?' Spynk asked. 'Will it have the prestige required for a council chamber?'

Michael was shocked.

'It's a Hopwood, as I explained, Mr Spynk, built to the glory of God,' he added uncharacteristically. Spynk almost looked at him.

'What is prestigious enough for the Almighty is not necessarily prestigious enough for a district councillor. They will need convincing, Michael, as I will. What are its acoustics, for instance? Does its long rectangular form suit its function? One would expect the seating to be arranged in a square or half-circle with members facing each other.'

'But that's adversarial!' Michael had expected this argument. 'It would be symbolic of politics in Glostover if all the members were facing the same way, let's call it east. The chancel, being on a higher level, is perfect for the chairman and his advisers.'

Spynk, he could see, remained sceptical. He diverted his attention to the main building where a more ergonomic logic had been applied. Each member of staff had been allocated an area based on the particular task he or she undertook. A word processor operator occupied x square metres, an engineer slightly more, an administrator somewhat less. Multi-purpose meetings rooms were provided for each section, thus reducing the dedicated floor space required. Spynk approved of this approach; it was the way he thought, ergonomically.

'And how do you propose to elevate the building?' he asked.

Michael visualised steep roofs, tapering chimneys and oriel windows; everything detailed in the elegant but functional style his paragon had perfected for keeping out the English weather.

'As Hopwood would have done it,' he said, 'the same treatment as the chapel. They would have to read together, don't you think?'

To Spynk, Hopwood was just another late Victorian architect. He was not overly familiar with the period, and even less fond.

'I hope,' he said reedily, 'that you are not intending to replicate Manchester's Town Hall among our leafy glades.'

'That was Waterhouse,' Michael corrected, 'and High Gothic Revival!'

'Whoever! It is you, not C. P. Hopkins, or Alfred Waterhouse, who will be drawing up this scheme. And you have two weeks to do it. Last night Council gave itself outline planning consent. A design sub-committee has been arranged for the nineteenth of this month. The credibility of the department is in your hands, Michael. Will you make it?' Michael collected the drawings together.

'I will if someone can give me a hand.' He thought about the teams in the other, larger drawing office, mainly technicians, some architectural assistants, as those whose training as architects had been ended by marriage, lack of money or of perseverance, were known. One of their number had become an architect through a long apprenticeship, as was possible in the years following the second world war. Spynk shook his head.

'All too busy with the housing capital programme, I'm afraid. You can have Ronnie Barge but he's the only one I can spare.'

'That's fine,' said Michael. 'Between us we'll do it, Mr Spynk.'

Be positive, Andrea always said. He was hardly through the door when self-doubt assailed him. Two weeks to design and draw up a multimillion-pound project? What had he let himself in for?

* * *

Maxwell Spynk leaned his elbows on the desk and formed a precise structure with his fingertips. He found these young men and their passion for past styles hard to understand. In schools of architecture in the early sixties he and his contemporaries had been taught the Modern Movement not as a style but as a philosophy, a religion even. It had arrived in Britain late, delayed by conservatism and the Second World War, its prophets, Gropius, Mies van der Rohe, le Corbusier, already approaching deification in other countries. He had answered its call.

It was Spynk's creed that *form followed function,* that *less was more.* He believed a house was *a machine for living in* as some believed the thoughts of Chairman Mao. No matter that the British public had never taken the movement to its heart;

he was a pioneer, the future was his, Maxwell Spynk's. What, after all, could be more up to date than Modern?

The advent of the Postmodern style caught Spynk like a Stalinist in Berlin when the Wall came down. His values were rejected. His contemporaries revised their pasts, young men sought old religions. But Spynk kept the faith. Never would a fibreglass clocktower adorn one of his buildings, or plaster arch within! He lived austerely on in the glass and concrete box he had built in nineteen seventy-two; alone since his wife had left him for Laura Ashley and a cottage in Wales.

Maxwell Spynk was out of his time. He waited for the world to come to its senses. *The glory of God,* indeed! He was more than a little concerned about young Maby!

That afternoon Michael went to see Geoff Lomax. The planner was not optimistic about the chances of the Hopwood chapel being listed, at least in the time available. The process took about six months if one was fortunate; there were forms to be filled, notices to be posted. Civil servants had to visit and write reports. Conservationists, he warned Michael, were not generally interested in anything which was not timber framed and leaning at least ten degrees from the vertical. History, they believed, ended at the accession of Victoria! He promised, however, to try, though he was very busy.

On Tuesday and Wednesday Michael interviewed the chief officers individually to explain how floorspace had been ergonomically apportioned within their departments. On Thursday and Friday, he altered the plans so that floorspace was related to salary grades. The meetings rooms became chief officers' suites. By fitting four-word processor operators into the space designated for three and reducing the number of toilets,

Michael managed to keep the increase in floorspace down to fifteen per cent. The schedule was maintained by working overtime. This met with the approval of Ronnie Barge whose grade was low enough to attract time and-a-half payment, but not that of Andrea who remained distinctly frosty all week.

It was late again on Friday evening when Michael turned into Falklands Drive. Couples were already drifting into the Jolly Huntsman. He almost joined them. Anticipation of Andrea's welcome and of another cauliflower cheese, both cold, brought alcohol to mind. The meal at least, he consoled himself, could be microwaved. He opened his front door, however, to the *Concierto d'Aranjuez* and the smell of something cooking in garlic.

'Down in a minute, pet,' Andrea called from upstairs, 'pour me a drink, will you?'

The dining table was laid for two, with their best cutlery and some pink napkins Michael had not seen since their wedding day. A fat candle reflected from glass and silverplate. Michael accessed his memory. It was not their anniversary, not Andrea's birthday, nor his. A minor anniversary, perhaps, the day they met, the first time they—! No, that was winter; he remembered how cold it had been in the back of the car.

He poured two dry sherries and rehearsed excuses. Lewisham's were right out of her favourite perfume/album/lingerie. They'd promised it would be here today. God, he'd been angry with them! He was on the point of rushing round to the late-night grocers when he heard Andrea descending the stairs.

'Hello, darling.' She paused in the doorway, reading his face for the effect she was having, which was considerable. She had made up, in the slightly overdone, slightly tarty way which brought colour to his face too. Her dress, white, insubstantial and clinging, promised all.

'Sorry I'm late,' he offered lamely, then inspirationally, 'but every florist in the town was closed. You wouldn't believe it, would you, with the recession and everything?'

Andrea smiled. 'So, you did remember.'

She took his lapels and pulled his mouth to hers. The concierto's strings burst forth with Iberian intensity. He was transported to a warm night charged with orange blossom and frying onions. Of course, their first holiday together, in Alicante! Over her shoulder he noticed an open bottle of Rioja glinting in the candlelight.

'How could I forget,' he murmured, nibbling her ear.

'That hungry, are we?' Andrea said.

She took her drink to the kitchen, leaving Michael to search the record rack for anything vaguely Spanish: Ravel, de Falla, *The Best of Los Bravos,* which someone had left after a party. He downed his sherry in one and dashed upstairs to shower. It took three minutes. Using a spray-on deodorant in front of the mirror, he found himself stamping out the flamenco, startling Andrea in the kitchen below.

He returned just as she was carrying the starter into the dining room. 'Artichokes a la Royal Institute,' Michael said, borrowing one of Arthur Brickbatt's jokes at his profession's expense.

'That's more like it,' Andrea said, 'you've been very serious lately. I suppose it's the job?'

Michael agreed it was. He did not want to talk about work tonight. He stripped a fleshy petal from his artichoke and fed it to her across the table, watching as she squeezed it between tongue and teeth. She fed one to him. Guitars smouldered on the Sony system.

'We ought to get out more,' Andrea said, 'see a bit of life.'

Michael nodded. He poured them a second glass of wine. How lovely Andrea looked in candlelight. He told her so. She squeezed his hand.

They ate paella to Ravel's *Boléro*, fastidiously at first but with progressively larger forkfuls as the tempo increased. A light fall of rice and small sea creatures littered the tablecloth.

'Torvil and Dean!' said Andrea.

'Bo Derek!' thought Michael. He squeezed her hand. Their feet touched under the table. He ran his ankle up and down her calf.

'Oliver rang earlier,' Andrea said. The music wavered, it seemed, then carried on. 'To ask us to a Ladies' Evening.'

'Does that mean you and Jane go to the pub while Oliver and I watch ice dancing on the box? Doesn't sound like the chauvinist I know and love.'

She giggled. 'You know perfectly well what it means. And you shouldn't be so hostile. He's only trying to help you get on in life.'

'Hmm.'

Andrea leaned across the table, her breasts brushing the remains of the paella. A shrimp peered from her cleavage.

'They're really good, these Pargetters' dos. And we haven't been out for ages. I'd really like to go.'

The candlelight shone from her pupils, now dilated, from the glasses and the wine bottle, now empty. Black is black, the new album proclaimed.

'Oh, all right,' Michael said.

By mutual consent they abandoned the dessert and Los Bravos. Some things would keep, some things would not.

A little later, as the sofa rocked gently on the Mediterranean and nightingales sang in a purple sky, Andrea said, 'I'll need a new dress, of course. I can have a new dress?'

There was a warm breeze from Africa too, and shooting stars, lots of them, over groves of olives.

'Yes,' said Michael. 'Yes, yes, yes – oh, yes!'

Chapter Five

The building used by Glostover District Council as its committee room had started life as a Congregational Sunday School. Despite several attempts to modernise it, an air of stern and scrubbed morality survived. Twelve-point-five millimetres of plasterboard and a half brick thickness separated the guardians of local democracy inside from the cold and traffic noise of the street, asbestos tiles and a sloping ceiling from the heavens. An antiquated heating system kept up a constant grumble on behalf of the ratepayers, belching magnificently at key points of members' speeches. The hall was rented out for other functions. In a cupboard at one end resided the instruments and pompoms of the Glostwich Junior Marching Band, commended Aberystwyth nineteen seventy-nine. A scrap of crimson tissue paper remained Blu-Tacked to the base of a collar truss since the playgroup's Christmas party of the same year. It fluttered in the draught from the ill-fitting windows.

In a suit and growing trepidation, Michael watched the Design Sub-Committee filing in through the door. He was sitting on the end of the raised dais which housed the council's officers, rising in status like the back row of a chessboard to the chairman and chief executive in the centre and falling again to the committee clerk at the other end. A large mobile board to his right displayed his drawings of the proposed civic centre. Some of the councillors examined the drawings as they entered, others waved at their political allies and mouthed jocular greetings across the room. In contrast to the besuited officers and to emphasise their representation of the common man, they wore comfortable jackets, sweaters and even open-necked shirts. Representatives of the common woman, though they would have baulked at the phrase, were better presented in flowery frocks and red lipstick. They all appeared to use the same hairdresser.

At seven o'clock precisely the chairman banged his gavel on the table and the chatter, guffaws and scraping of chairs rumbled to a halt. This was an auspicious night, he informed the assembly, tonight they were to consider the design of a building which would have a profound impact on the district of Glostover for generations to come. He glared at two members who were still whispering in the second row. The word *fairway* had been distinctly heard.

'We have with us from the Architects' Section,' the chairman continued, 'Mr Maby, who will explain the scheme and answer any questions you may have.' Heads turned curiously in Michael's direction; it was not often that the spotlight fell on an officer of his lowly grade. Michael smiled weakly and started to rise.

'But before he does so!' Michael sat down again. 'I would emphasise that we are discussing the *design* and not the siting. The choice of Fairybridge Court has already been made by Policy and Finance Committee.' There was an outbreak of grumbling from the minority party who had been out-manoeuvred as foretold at the meeting of the brotherhood. 'Mr Maby!'

'Thank you, Chairman.' Michael rose for a second time. His lower lip felt three inches thick. At the end of the row in front of him and as far to the left as possible without sitting in the porch, the Council's one Socialist winked in encouragement. He drank in the Jolly Huntsman.

'The inspiration for this scheme,' Michael began on a high note, higher than intended, 'is the former chapel of Fairybridge Court, in which it is proposed the Council Chamber should be housed. We are almost certain that the chapel was designed by the architect, C. P. Hopwood.' He pointed out the photographs. The faces of the Design Sub-Committee remained blank. 'It will be refurbished to an authentic high standard and—' he consulted his notes desperately, 'have a roof put on it.'

'That's a good idea,' said the Socialist. Michael reeled off the other improvements he had listed. In rehearsal it had seemed to take longer.

'Which brings me to the main building.' He introduced with his open left hand the plans and elevations on the board behind him. It was a gesture he had borrowed from the weather presenters on television, and it generated the same response from his audience as tidings of an approaching depression.

'This will accommodate all the Council's staff. It has been elevated to respect the style of the chapel and its plan form uses another Hopwood device, being laid out in the form of a letter, in this case F for Fairybridge.' A G-plan for Glostover, Michael had found, produced excessive corridors. He explained to the sub-committee how Hopwood had adopted the device from sixteenth-century Catholics who used symbolic letter plans for their houses as an act of defiance. Their defiance would have been more impressive, Ronnie Barge had said, if the Protestants had had spy-planes.

The faint murmur of interest in the plan form died away as Michael went through the detailed arrangement of the departments, the computer room and the printing section. Yawns were stifled; someone at the back had his eyes closed. He jerked awake as his chin met his chest. Michael finished with an explanation of the basement carpark and the lawns which it would facilitate, surrounding the building and stretching away, over a ha-ha perhaps, into parkland revitalised for the enjoyment of the people of Glostwich. He stood back, moderately pleased with his performance. Were there any questions?

'What about the heating?' This from Councillor Tudge who had recently installed bottled gas heating in his mother's bungalow and welcomed the opportunity to air his newly acquired knowledge of BTUs and 'U' values. He did so until stopped by the chairman. Michael promised that bottled gas would be considered when they reached that stage. He then had to explain to Councillor Mrs Mortar why the basement carpark did not appear on the elevations. And anyway, opined Mrs Mortar, of Mortars' Motors, what was wrong with cars that you had to bury them underground?

The Labour member asked if using the F-plan would necessitate extra toilets. Some of the ladies tutted. It was the sort of joke they would expect from a socialist. He also asked how ratepayers without cars were expected to get to Fairybridge and its one-stop-shop but was ruled out of order.

'We're here to talk about aesthetics!' said Councillor Warren, the greengrocer from Glostwich High Street. He liked that word, *aesthetics,* and used it on every possible occasion. 'Now I'm not sure about this Victorian stuff, Georgian's more in my line. It's not as if this Hopkins bloke is famous. If he'd been a well-known artitett, like Christopher Wren or ...'

'Basil Spence,' someone assisted him.

'It might have been different!'

'I agree with Councillor Warren,' a silver-haired man in a blazer interposed. At the sound of his voice would-be speakers lowered their hands. Robert Snow had been a councillor for less than a year but already some thought of him as a future Leader. The Groat faction despised him. He had been on the board of a pharmaceutical company but had left, it was rumoured, with a large settlement after a hostile merger. Councillor Snow believed that the few local government workers who were necessary should be housed in Nyssen huts. He had presented papers on the squandering of British public funds to conferences from Singapore to Rio.

'What concerns me,' said Councillor Snow, 'is the cost of this elaborate architecture! Mr Maby has not yet mentioned what should be our primary concern, the amount of public money this venture is going to swallow up.' He glanced at the girl from the *Bugle*, scribbling in the corner.

Michael opened his mouth and closed it again. The estimated cost of the project was included in the agenda; he had been instructed to keep off the subject. The treasurer stepped in; he had years of experience in the art of confusing committees and proceeded to use it. After ten minutes of rate support grants, revolving funds and ring-fencing, the Design Sub-Committee was mesmerised. Councillor Snow, however, was made of sterner stuff.

'I fully understand the finances,' he persisted, 'what I am asking Mr Maby is how much less the project would cost if a more functional style was adopted.'

A wave of panic rose from Michael's stomach and surged through his brain. The quantity surveyor's figures were not interpretable in that way. An admission of ignorance would make him appear foolish. He was about to guess at a minor saving, when Maxwell Spynk spoke from further along the dais.

'If I may, Chairman?' He addressed the fluttering Christmas decoration on the roof truss. 'I would like to emphasise that this is a preliminary design and has, for the best of reasons, been strongly influenced by the existence of the chapel. It has yet to be proved that the chapel was designed by Hopwood. It may well be that, as detailed design proceeds, a more functional treatment will emerge. Approval of the layout is all we ask at present.'

The compromise met the sub-committee's approval. It was getting late. The vote was seventeen *for,* one *against* and two abstentions, the socialist and the man asleep on the back row. The members left for the Glendower Arms or, in two cases, for the arms of each other. As Michael took down the elevations he had laboured over for seven days and nights, the boiler rumbled like distant laughter.

* * *

Michael slept badly that night. For hours he continued to address the Design Sub-Committee, humiliating Councillor Snow with sharp one-liners, lecturing Councillor Warren on greengrocery. Cats mated in the garden; Andrea's every snort and shift beside him brought him instantly awake. His normal foetal position failed to bring comfort, as did its reverse and a stomach down spell. Cramp vied with indigestion from his late dinner.

He had been lying on his back for some time, like an entombed crusader, when he gradually became aware of a cloud forming over the end of the bed, a pinkish cloud in the shape of a sun-lounger. A translucent figure reposed upon it. It was bearded and anatomically precise. The naked children of Princess Margaret Gardens hovered in attendance, rudimentary wings sprouting from their shoulders. Michael recognized, with no great surprise, the god-like features of Charles Pericles Hopwood.

The apparition reached out a languid arm. He stretched to meet it and their fingers touched. Something like electricity passed between them.

'You have done well, Michael,' the apparition mouthed. The sound followed out of synch. 'And I am here to help you. Come!'

Michael climbed aboard the cloud, a cherub at each elbow. The duvet trailed behind him like a robe. They looked down on the exposed form of Andrea, sprawled artlessly on the bed, and the apparition sighed, a long and longing sigh. Then they were off, speeding through the night sky, the lights of Glostwich winking far below them.

'What does it do to the gallon?' Michael asked by way of conversation. They looped the loop. It beat Oliver's new motor hands down.

In no time at all they reached Fairybridge, passing straight through the chapel's west window. The stained glass reassembled behind them. Michael noted its non-biblical theme, the quest for the Holy Grail, the pale, red-haired damsels and the brilliant golds and greens which blazed around Sir Galahad. As they landed a rotund figure in waistcoat and bowler looked up from the pew he was carving.

'Good day, Mr Hopwood, sir.' He scrambled to his feet.

'Morning, Pugh,' the apparition replied absently, looking round at the tiles being laid and the ironwork wrought. He had changed into tweeds and a deerstalker. 'This is my new provisional assistant, Mr Maby.'

Pugh touched his bowler. 'Let us hope it becomes confirmed, sir,' he said. 'May I conduct you both round the works? I believe all will be finished within the month.'

They followed him round the chapel, examining piers and pilasters, floating to the top of the rood screen to inspect the quality of carving. There was a smell of new stone and sawdust, the persistent tap of mallet on chisel. C.P. issued instructions, which Pugh recorded in a leather-bound book. Michael too had a book, in which he made immaculate sketches of the detailing with amazing speed. He showed them to C.P., who smiled paternally.

'That's my boy,' he said, and Michael swelled with pride. They were standing on the chancel steps when C.P.'s mobile phone rang. It was some Viceroy. 'A client, must go,' C.P. said and began to fade. His voice went first. Before he disappeared altogether, he took Michael's sketch pad and wrote something in it. Then Pugh imploded. There was a chorus of boos from the Design Sub-Committee seated in the nave.

'Typical builder,' said Councillor Tudge, 'always disappear when you need them.'

Michael restarted his presentation. 'The quality of mercy is not strained,' he said, 'it droppeth as the gentle rain from heaven.' He noticed that the sub-committee had raised umbrellas and, looking up, that the roof had gone. The chapel reverted to a ruin before his eyes. He raised an heroic tee square. 'And close the wall up with our English dead!'

The sub-committee, by now the size of a small army, bayed furiously. Michael walked through it down the aisle, with as much dignity as the wearing of just a pyjama top would allow. He ran home semi-naked across the town, behind him a pack of large women in violet housecoats in hot pursuit.

* * *

'You had a bad night, didn't you?' Andrea said grumpily. She pulled at the duvet which Michael held tight up to his chin. He was sweating.

The jerk of the duvet caused something white to fall to the floor, a sketch pad. He picked it up and thumbed through the sheets. To his disappointment there were no architectural details. On a centre page, however, and in a strange and esoteric hand five words were written. He deciphered them aloud.

'What was that?' Andrea mumbled into her pillow.

'Beware the birds of prey,' he repeated.

Chapter Six

During the next few weeks, Michael and Ronnie Barge worked hard on the detailed design plans, interrupted daily with advice by Maxwell Spynk. The gypsy site and various modernisation schemes with which Ronnie had been involved had been handed to other staff. Their drawing boards faced each other, Ronnie's equipped with parallel motion, Michael preferring the traditional tee square. The drawings were done on A1 sheets of tracing paper, stuck to the boards with strips of masking tape. Michael drew the plans lightly in pencil and Ronnie inked them in, swearing profusely when the finer nibs of his rapidograph clogged up and he had to wash them out at the sink. Then Michael turned to the elevational treatment, in his mind the style of C. P. Hopwood.

According to Geoff Lomax, the attempt to have the chapel listed had run into difficulties. English Heritage were distinctly sceptical; a latticed column and carved initials did not constitute proof of the building's pedigree in their eyes, even if Hopwood had been in the right place at the right time. Michael realised he needed further evidence to ensure its protection.

He took a Friday off, fitting in with Andrea's shifts, and they took the train to London. 'Don't worry about me,' Ronnie Barge encouraged him. He'd cope with Spynk, and the phone calls. Ronnie had no leave left; he took all his as early as possible in the year in case he died and missed out. 'I'll manage,' he said.

Andrea was in London for the shopping, notably for the dress Michael had rashly promised for the Pargetters' do. She swept through the West End, blitzing boutiques, decimating department stores. Michael trailed behind her, six steps on the escalators, a full spin in the revolving doors. He stood sheepishly in changing areas, striving to avoid glimpses of flesh through the curtains which surrounded him on two sides and their reflections in a mirrored third. Raising his eyes from a display of French knickers, he met the gaze of the shop assistant. Did he prefer the sage or the aubergine, she asked.

Andrea's choice eventually narrowed to the first dress she had tried on in Oxford Street, blue, and the little black number which she was currently wearing. Michael liked that one, he told her. The shop assistant agreed: black was always flattering; not that madam needed to be flattered! Madam settled on the blue dress from Oxford Street.

The accessories, Andrea felt, she could choose without Michael's help. He could go and do whatever it was he had to do; she would meet him later. With a sinking feeling he departed. He had not reckoned on accessories. He was still feeling anxious as he walked between the twin phalluses that guarded the entrance to number 66, Portland Place. But then, the Royal Institute of British Architects had always had that effect on him.

'Always nice to see members from the provinces,' the receptionist said as he signed in. This before he had entered his address. He climbed the black marble stairs, under the scrutiny of past presidents, pausing to peer into the first-floor hall where he and generations of other students had been interrogated, its hardwood floor protected from their nasty provincial feet and pencil-sharpenings by a vast tarpaulin. The inquisitorial faces of oral examiners materialised before him. 'So, what would you say are the implications of Clause 8, par 7:2:3, Mr Maby?' Butterflies awoke from hibernation in Mr Maby's stomach.

The library had much on Hopwood's middle and late periods, the great country houses, the government buildings for Kuala Lumpur, never built. Some of his original drawings were housed there, yellowing gracefully. Michael spent more time than he could afford admiring the immaculate draughtsmanship, tracing the path of the master's hand with his own, over the glass which protected it. The librarian looked sternly at him on more than one occasion.

Of the early years, however, there was little of relevance. The quarrel with Gosplett, and Hopwood's subsequent wilderness year were documented. Apparently, he had wandered Scandinavia for several months, sketching stave churches and Viking artefacts, before returning to resume his career in England. Fairybridge Court was not mentioned anywhere.

Michael was thinking it was time he headed for the tube when the little brass plaque on the frame of the Kuala Lumpur drawing caught his eye. *Donated by his daughter, Dora, b.1907.* Donated, not bequeathed! Was it possible? He borrowed a directory of members from the librarian. Had Dora not been an architect too? He found her in the list of honorary members. *Dora Hopwood-Brown.* There was an address in Herefordshire.

He had to race for the tube. By the time he reached Paddington, Andrea was pacing up and down outside the ticket barrier. They just made it. The accessories turned out to be shoes, a gold bag, necklace, earrings and an angora wrap in case it was cold. It seemed ungracious to ask the cost.

* * *

'For God's sake, Ronnie, what on earth have you done?' It was Monday morning and Michael was standing by his colleague's board, aghast. Before he had left the office on the previous Thursday, he had given Ronnie his pencilled sheet depicting the south-west and north-east elevations of the Fairybridge scheme, to be inked in. These showed the canopied entrance door, the steeply pitched gables and overhanging eaves supported at intervals by light iron stays, with a tapering chimney stack rising above them carrying the fumes from the boiler house far below. These had all gone. In their place was a flat roof.

'Don't blame me,' said Ronnie. 'It was Spynky. I told him you wouldn't like it!'

'Too right, I wouldn't like it.' Michael headed for the door.

'You sort him out, mate,' Ronnie said, shaking his 0.2 mm rapidograph which had clogged up again over the weekend, 'and the best of British luck!'

Spynk was expecting him. He put aside the document he was reading and placed his hands together sanctimoniously on the desk between them.

'Sit down, Michael.' He paused to let Michael comply.

'It's about Fairybridge Court, Mr Spynk, I—'

Spynk held up a cautionary hand.

'Let me say, firstly, Michael, that I have no issues with the plans you have come up with, which seem to be entirely logical. However, you are basing your elevational treatment on the ruins of a chapel, allegedly designed by an Arts and Crafts architect at the turn of this century, when skilled labour was relatively inexpensive. May I remind you we are less than ten years away from the millennium and should be designing in an appropriately modern manner. In the absence of any official recognition of the pedigree of your chapel, I must insist that the main building is considered independently.' He reached for his document again.

'But the restoration of the chapel itself, for use as the Council Chamber, Mr Spynk, will still proceed, will it not?'

'We shall see, Michael, we shall see.'

Michael returned to the drawing office and slumped over his board with his head in his hands.

'How did the sort out go then?' asked Ronnie.

* * *

The address given for Dora Hopwood-Brown in the members' directory was a private nursing home on the banks of the Wye. Michael wrote to her that evening and received a telephone call towards the end of the week from the matron. Mrs Hopwood-Brown would be pleased to see him for afternoon tea on Sunday.

To his surprise Andrea decided to come with him. They made a day of it and had a pub lunch on the way, dawdling down wooded lanes, even stopping for a walk. Wyebrae stood on a promontory overlooking the river at the end of an avenue of limes. Sunlight filtered through their leaves.

They were shown to the terrace, with wrought iron furniture and a stone balustrade. Below them the river murmured over a shelf of hard rock.

'Bet the fees are high here,' Andrea whispered.

After some minutes a French window opened, and a nurse backed out with a wheelchair in tow. The old lady in it had thin white hair and was wrapped from ankle to waist in a tartan blanket.

'Are you sure you'll be warm enough, Mrs Hopwood-Brown?' the nurse asked.

'You'll be the first to know if I'm not,' the old lady said sharply. She winked at them. 'Got to keep them on their toes; the fees are high enough.' Her skin was rhino-hide, but her eyes darted like tick birds. She scrutinised Andrea's face and her ring finger. Michael introduced them both.

'As I said in my letter,' he began. The old lady interrupted him.

'And children, Mrs Maby, do you have children?'

'No,' said Andrea.

'Not yet,' Michael added.

'Don't leave it too late,' said Mrs Hopwood-Brown. 'I never had any. Too busy with my first marriage, too old with my second. At least, he was. You'd think an architect would have lead in his pencil, wouldn't you?'

Andrea giggled. Michael was taken aback, this the daughter of an icon.

'I wrote about your father, Mrs Hopwood-Brown. I'm a great admirer.'

'The old devil's back in fashion, is he? Always thought it was old hat myself. All those fussy mouldings, labour intensive arty-crafty stuff. I'm of the Bauhaus generation, clean lines, no nonsense.'

Michael explained about the chapel. The old lady listened, her sharp eyes at the same time noting Andrea's wandering attention, her stifled yawn.

'Sounds like Poppa!' she said when he had finished. 'But well before my time, of course. I was the baby of the family, youngest of eight. By the time I was old enough to notice he was designing the grand Imperial stuff. Pomp and circumstance, you know.'

The matron came out with a tray of tea and biscuits. It was not her line of work, but she liked to make sure that visitors were given a favourable impression of life at Wyebrae, and Mrs Hopwood-Brown could be difficult. She smiled encompassingly as she poured.

'Mrs Maby's a physiotherapist, she'd sort you out,' the old lady said.

'Now, Dora,' the matron chided. She nodded a shared understanding at Andrea. 'Would you like to see over the accommodation, Mrs Maby? We're rather proud of it.'

Andrea accepted the invitation, already on her feet. She took her tea with her, turning back for two custard creams, then following the matron through the French window.

'Quite a stunner, your wife. You make sure you don't lose her.' The old lady eyed Michael shrewdly. 'She doesn't share your interests, does she?'

'Well, no!' Michael admitted. 'But that's not everything, is it?'

'It's a good percentage of everything, Mr Maby, if you take the passion away.'

He found himself confiding in this octogenarian, telling her his story, his ambitions. He liked her. There was none of the tension that was always there with younger women. She was direct but receptive. It was three-quarters of an hour before he remembered that he was supposed to be interviewing her.

'I can't recall anything about a chapel at Glostwich,' she said when pressed. 'And I have a good memory still! However, my older sister had some papers of Poppas, which were passed to me when she died, five years ago. They're still with the solicitor. I confess I have never read them. If it helps, I will instruct him to show them to you.' She dismissed his thanks.

'Now tell me, what do you think of Michael Atherton, Mr Maby? I'm willing to bet he'll take over the England captaincy next season. Goochy can't last forever. I just hope the responsibility doesn't compromise his batting. That happens sometimes, you know.' Michael nodded wisely. He knew nothing about cricket.

When they were leaving and the nurse was wheeling her indoors, she called him back.

'Let me give you some advice, Michael. Stop living in the past! You've time enough for that when you're my age. Myself, I prefer the future. Now don't take me back to the common room, nurse. They'll all be watching *Songs of Praise*.'

* * *

'Andrea,' Michael said as they drove back to Glostwich, 'do you think we ought to be trying for a baby?'

Andrea looked at him in alarm. 'Good Lord, no! When we have a decent house and you have a better job, maybe!' She saw his face fall.

'But we can practice, if you like.'

Chapter Seven

The rituals and regalia of regular Pargetters' meetings were all but abandoned on Ladies' Nights. Women, it was considered, were too prosaic to appreciate ceremony, nor could their discretion be relied upon. Secrecy was a masculine attribute. On Ladies' Nights, therefore, the ceremonial haversacks were left at home, the robes replaced by dinner jackets. The only insignia displayed were the silver lapel-badges, miniaturised replicas of the pargetter's trowel and worn by all brethren, from the grand chancellor to the lowest journeyman, on the side above the heart. Rank was suspended for the night.

At the centre of the long table on the opposite side of the dancefloor from the band, the grand chancellor of the Church Newington Kiln, which was hosting the regional dinner this year, surveyed the room with satisfaction. On all sides the tradesmen and professionals of the region conversed socially over the fish course. Most, like him, were past the athletic stage, the men's bulges restrained by cummerbunds, their wives' figures made indistinguishable by elaborate folds of shiny material. Here and there, however, a sharp hairstyle or a slim bare shoulder testified to his policy of initiating younger members. He lingered particularly over a blonde girl who appeared to be a guest of that promising Doctor Harrington, Oliver, was it not? He passed over the young man next to her.

The young man next to her ran a finger round the collar of his hired dress shirt. His trousers, also from Moss Bros, were on the tight side too. It had been that or overlong legs. He finished his salmon and glanced sideways at Andrea, in laughing conversation with Oliver opposite and the regional sales manager of Orifice Plumbing Products to her right.

'Yes, I really miss the Eighties,' the regional sales manager was saying, 'we have to project a caring image these days. My company's sponsoring water supplies in M'boto now. The house magazine's full of grateful natives hanging around the standpipe with buckets!'

On the other side of the table Jane was being polite to a gentlemen's outfitter. His wife, next to Michael, regarded the conversation, Jane's bosom and the cutlery with equal disdain. She was encased in gold brocade. He felt obliged to speak to her.

'Did you come last year?' he asked.

'My husband and I,' said the gentlemen's outfitter's wife, 'have been attending these functions for the last thirty years. They are not what they once were!'

Michael finished his Muscadet. He adjusted his tie.

A good gent's sock, the outfitter informed Jane, required suspenders.

'Ought to support themselves, if you ask me,' said the regional sales manager, 'stand on their own two feet!'

The fish course was followed by *medallions de boeuf*, with carrots, broccoli and baked potatoes. The *boeuf* had, it seemed, been awarded its *medallions* for long service. Several glasses of red wine, however, hastened its departure. Michael endured the meal on the fringe of two conversations, passed from time to time a wink from Oliver, the horse-radish sauce or one of Jane's

lovely smiles. He tried again with the gentlemen's outfitter's wife.
Holidays were always a good topic. Her last one, however, had
been in 1979. Assistants, evidently, could not be relied upon to
take care of the shop.

'Especially that floozy he's taken on!' she said grimly across
the table.

Her husband choked on a baked potato.

'What line of business are you in, Mr Maby?' he asked
hurriedly. Michael told him. 'With the Council,' he forestalled
the next question, 'at the moment.'

He poured himself another wine. No, someone else dealt with
refuse collections, he was afraid. Yes, the service would probably
be privatised.

The Black Forest gateau was the texture of damp sawdust
with cream from an aerosol, the coffee thin. Michael was relieved
when someone at the top table banged a gavel on it.

'Gentlemen, the Queen!' The Pargetters rose as a man.

'The Queen and Saint Bronwyn,' they responded.

'Bronwyn,' Oliver informed his guests as they sat down again,
'was the patron saint of Pargetters. Something to do with the
miraculous reversal of a flash plaster set in the fifteenth century.'

The ruddy man at the top table said a few words and introduced
their guest speaker, grand chancellor of the Glostwich Kiln and
chairman of Glostover District Council, Marcus Groat, who
would speak on 'The Rewards of Public Service'. Oh, my God,
thought Michael. He ignored a nudge from Andrea. *Look,* the
nudge said, *there's your big chance to make friends and influence
people!* He sank a little further into his seat.

His gloom was premature. Marcus Groat was of the *which
reminds me* school of after-dinner speaking. 'The Rewards of

Public Service' proved to be the slender thread on which a series of
otherwise unconnected jokes were strung, little gems, suggestive
without being lewd, mildly xenophobic. He knew his audience
well. Political correctness had yet to permeate the Pargetters.

'Which reminds me,' said the Groat, 'of the Pakistani
shopkeeper—'

Michael knew that one. It was one of Ronnie Barge's, another
example of his assistant being a step ahead of the Council.
Only that day he had learned of the secret moves to sell off the
Glostwich Library. He drained his glass and watched the faces
around him, smiles stretched to breaking point in anticipation
of the punchline.

'Two cases of Pal and a steak for the dog!'

A roar of released laughter filled the room, tables were slapped.
The regional sales manager was in tears, though he had heard
the joke several times before. He gasped for breath. The lips of
the gentlemen's outfitter's wife twitched slightly.

There was more. Marcus Groat was reminded of fourteen
stories during his half-hour speech. He was a natural. By the
end of it, Michael was laughing with the rest of them. A relaxed,
outgoing feeling began to steal over him. So outgoing was he
indeed, that he found himself leading a surprised Andrea onto the
dance floor before the end of the band's first number. Normally
he would have held out for at least thirty minutes.

Show me the way to Amarillo. The band, identified diagonally
across its speakers as Starshine, bounced its way through the first
number. It was followed by more hits from the previous two
decades. The two girl singers, courageous in lurex miniskirts,
would have heard their older sisters, possibly their mothers,
singing these songs. The keyboard player, doubling as male

vocalist, had bought the 45s. He and the bass guitarist were founder members of the band. During the day he made dentures.

On the floor middle-aged couples twitched and gyrated in stiff parodies of the movements of their youths; *the twist, the stomp, the mashed potato too,* thumbs stuck in belts, arms in the air, Travoltas, Jaggers and headbangers. Lasers stabbed the darkness, teeth shone purple in ultra-violet light. From the tables, the even more middle-aged watched with disapproval. But Michael felt other eyes on Andrea, stunning in electric blue. He danced like a bantam cock.

At the end of the warm-up session the keyboard player announced his intention of slowing the tempo down. The band broke into a foxtrot or something. As Michael and Andrea returned to their table, they met the outfitters poised for launch-off, elbows extended like bowsprits. 'Real dancing,' the man proclaimed. They caught the current and billowed out into the mainstream, Jane and Oliver in their wake. 'Pint of lager and a spritzer,' Oliver called over Jane's shoulder. What they were doing was not a foxtrot.

Michael went to the bar. The crush was three deep. It took him ten minutes to reach the front and five to catch the barmaid's eye. She took a further five minutes with the order and gave his change to the man next to him. Not that the change was worth having! He struggled back to the ballroom with a tray of drinks to find Andrea had gone.

In the darkness Marcus Groat steered the blonde girl through the crowd. For all his bulk he was still an accomplished dancer. He had spotted her during his speech, next to the young man who looked vaguely familiar. She was not practised but she followed his steps with skill. She was warm and pliant against him. It was one of his more agreeable duties, this squiring of potential journeymen's women. No grand chancellor in living memory had completed the ritual, but it excited Groat to know in theory he could, that every Pargetter in the room knew the rule that said he could. He slid his hand down her back and drew her against his abdomen. Her smile never faltered.

Michael had all but finished his pint of warm keg bitter by the time that Groat returned Andrea to the table. There had been little else to do but drink.

'I think you know each other,' Andrea said.

'Yes, of course,' Michael said. Groat looked doubtful. 'Glostover District Council, the Architects' Section?' Michael prompted. Recognition dawned on Groat's face.

'Ah, yes, you're the young man who's designing my new offices. Well done, well done! Should do you a power of good. All progressing, I trust?'

'Well, yes.' Michael said, 'I'm having some trouble getting the chapel listed, but I'm still working on it.' He smiled in a confident, professional manner.

'The chapel? Ah yes, the derelict chapel.' Groat leered at Andrea. 'You're a lucky man, Malcolm, a lucky man!' Michael was taken aback.

'I suppose I am, sir, being a Hopwood disciple, so to speak!'

'Hmm?' Groat said absently. Inspiration struck his architect.

'I don't suppose,' Michael said, 'that you have any documents about the original buildings; you being the owner of the land and all?'

The smile left Groat's face abruptly. His piggy eyes narrowed.

'My land, young man? You must be misinformed. The land belongs to my wife's family. I have no pecuniary interest at all.' His smile returned. 'And thinking about my wife, I see her beckoning. Nice to meet you, Mrs Mulvey.'

He excused himself.

'All that groping I put up with, and you cocked it up!' Andrea said angrily.

'What groping?'

'Never mind!'

'Ready for a drink?' Oliver asked.

From that point onward Michael's night became increasingly confused. That Andrea was annoyed with him he knew; why, he was unsure. She danced with the regional sales manager, the gentlemen's outfitter and with Oliver, on several occasions, but not with him. He danced with Jane. He narrowly escaped the gentlemen's outfitter's wife by dashing to the bar. It was not even his round. Then he danced with Jane again.

Andrea would come around, Jane thought. She had always been mercurial. Did he remember that time at college when—Yes, he remembered! They talked about old times as they shuffled round the dance floor. *Lady in red,* crooned the dental technician. They laughed, for Jane was wearing scarlet. This would always be their song Michael told her, in a Noel Coward sort of voice. He sang along tunelessly in her ear: *The way you look tonight.* She was soft and reassuring against him. Somehow, he forgot about Andrea.

Later he found himself sitting alone with Oliver. The ladies had gone to powder their noses.

'You fancy Jane, don't you?' Oliver said. Michael protested.

'It's all right. I fancy Andrea too, always have.'

They eyed each other over the hoard of empty glasses. Michael felt a guilty smile creep over his face. Suddenly they were both laughing.

'It's just not natural, marriage,' Oliver was finally able to say, 'at the end of the day men are polygamous.'

'Pogymalous!' Michael agreed.

They drank to pogymaly. Beer ran down Michael's chin and onto his hired shirt and tie.

'Here,' Oliver passed him a handkerchief. He was not such a bad bloke.

'Trouble is,' he said, 'you go having affairs, next thing you know it's the divorce courts. Lose your house, lose your car, split the record collection. Just not worth it!'

'And the china,' Michael said, searching for a contribution.

'If it hasn't been thrown at you. And you can't pay for favours, can you? God knows what you'd get!' They drank some more beer.

'A dose,' Michael remembered the term.

'At least!' Oliver said. 'I'm sure the best approach is to be honest about it. After all, women must like a change of scene too. Why not allow each other a bit of freedom? With someone of like mind, someone you both know,' he added.

Michael acknowledged the logic of this. They were quiet for a moment. *I just called to say I love you,* sang the girls in the band, *I just called to say how much I care.*

'Have you and Andrea ever thought of—?' Oliver asked.

'Oh, no,' Michael said. It was at least half untrue. However, his curiosity got the better of him. 'How about you?'

'Now and again.' Oliver lit a cigar. 'Why don't we try it?' Michael ogled him. The drifting smoke added to the sense of unreality.

'You sherious?'

'Why not? We're all grown-ups, we all know each other. Add a touch of spice to your marriage. What could be wrong with that?'

Michael struggled with his dispersing senses. At the far end of
the room, he could see the girls emerging from the toilet door and
beginning to walk towards them, his wife, blonde and beautiful,
her dark-haired friend, equally lovely, though in a gentler way.
Plain, Jane was manifestly not.

'Naah,' he said, 'Andrea would never agree to anything like
that.'

* * *

Michael sat out the last dance. His legs, he felt, had done enough.
He watched the throng surging past the table in the darkness,
occasionally in focus, Oliver with Andrea, the Sales Manager
with Jane. *The last waltz should last forever,* the keyboard player
sang insincerely. He had to be up early the next morning; the
local dentist had a run on bridges. *Goodnight,* the men's outfitter
said as he passed, *See you next year.* His wife adjusted her fur
stole. She almost smiled. Waitresses began clearing the tables.
The lights came on.

It had been a good move to book rooms for the night. They
tumbled out of the lift on the third floor, laughing and shushing
each other.

'Champagne, everyone?' Oliver invited, dangling his room-
key over their heads.

'Not for me, I'm wanna go to bed.' Michael meandered down
the corridor.

'Nothing if not direct!' Oliver said.

They stopped outside room 314.

'I'm going to have a drink,' Andrea said. She nestled up to
Michael and looked into his eyes. 'It is alright, isn't it?'

'Courshe it is,' Michael said. If people wanted to drink it was their lookout. He knew when he had had enough. He managed to locate the lock with his key.

'Don't be long,' he called after them.

'Get him,' Oliver said.

Before he was in the room Michael had his tie off. The dinner jacket and trousers quickly followed it into the corner. He stumbled into the bathroom in his shirt, peed, splashed water on his face, stumbled out again and fell on the bed. The bedhead switch was within reach. He switched it off, but the bathroom light was still on. *Damn!* He closed his eyes. The room, predictably, started spinning, slowly at first then faster. He opened his eyes again and stared very hard at a ventilator grille until it stopped. He tried to keep awake. He drowsed. Somewhere, far away, a key turned in a lock. The music of the band still beat in his head.

Suddenly he smelt perfume. She stood by the bed looking down at him. In the light from the bathroom her dress was red. She slipped out of it.

'I'm not sure that this is a good idea,' she said.

He held back the duvet and she slid in beside him. For some moments he lay still, unsure whether this was real or a drunken delusion. Then he raised himself on an elbow and looked down on her face. Well, faces really, two of them. He made his choice, kissing her on the ear. She raised her body to him, just as a wave of nausea hit him. He rushed for the bathroom.

And that was it! He spent most of the night in there, hugging the lavatory pan. At five-thirty he crept back to lie alongside a sleeping partner. At eight he woke again next to Andrea. His head was throbbing.

Chapter Eight

The Central Area Planning Committee, to which the final design was to be presented, approached rapidly. Because of the urgency, Michael had been forced to accept the increasing involvement of Maxwell Spynk who, frustrated by his largely administrative role, relished being a designer once again. The original Hopwoodian features of Michael's design had long since disappeared under Spynk's flat roof, only the white rendered walls surviving. Trying to compensate for the reduction in visual interest, Michael had taken a reluctant step towards modernity and introduced large floor to ceiling windows on the ground floor, diminishing slightly on the first floor and again on the second. The glass was emphasised on the elevations with a film of pale Letratone, and shadows introduced to give depth to the two-dimensional drawing. Other transfers were added, of cars and people, pushing prams or conversing in a friendly manner outside the main entrance. Skeletal winter trees were placed carefully to disguise weaker points of the design.

Michael was more interested in the chapel. He intended to repair the walls and gables with local stone and top them with a kingpost timber roof covered in Welsh slate. A glazed bridge would run from its original entrance, over an inlet of the lake to the first floor of the main building, allowing pedestrians but not cars to pass under it. The round aperture in the west gable would be filled with a stained glass rose window, one of Hopwood's signature features. Michael had discovered a local glass artist with whom he was discussing, in his own time, a design depicting Sir Galahad and the Quest for the Holy Grail, a secular theme nodding at the building's original function.

Marital relations had regressed to their pre-shopping trip state. The Pargetters' evening and its climax, though that was hardly the word, had not been mentioned since. Michael veered between anger at Oliver's duplicity, shame that he had succumbed to it and mortification that he had failed to take advantage of it. He was unsure whether Andrea's coldness was because of his failure or because of his perceived part in the plot. What, indeed, had been Andrea's part in the plot? Or it's consummation? At what point had she returned to their room? Like an ostrich, he buried his head in his work.

Two weeks after their meeting at Wyebrae, he received a letter from Hopwood's daughter, Dora.

Dear Mr Maby, it read in a surprisingly firm hand, *I have instructed my solicitors, Goodman and Drew of Shrewsbury, to give you sight of Poppa's papers. Hope you'll find them useful.* A comprehensive criticism of the Test and County Cricket Board followed. *Keep your end up, Dora Hopwood-Brown.*

He rang Shrewsbury, then booked the following day off. Andrea was too busy to accompany him this time.

He found the solicitors' offices in a Georgian townhouse, just off the city centre in a quiet backwater. Messrs. Goodman and Drew Senior had long since passed to eternity, after lengthy delays, it was said locally, by St Peter's legal advisers. Mr Drew Junior offered him a trembling hand and a drink. He looked disappointed when Michael chose coffee.

'Are you a relative, Mr Maby?' he asked. Michael explained his interest.

'Dashed fine woman, Mrs Hopwood-Brown. Looked tremendous in a tennis skirt, wielding a racket, striding the base line.' His eyes glazed over. 'Of course, I was only a boy at the time.'

'You visited the family home, then?' Michael asked.

'Oh, yes! With my father, you know. Only met the great man once; he was usually abroad. It was a garden party, just before he died. Lots of right honourables, viscounts, maharajahs, beautiful ladies. He gave me a peach, picked it off the wall for me. Looked like a God!'

'I know,' Michael said. Mr Drew peered at him over half-lens glasses.

'From the photographs,' Michael said hurriedly, 'did your father have any stories?'

'Oh, yes!' Mr Drew recounted a marginally interesting tale about C.P. and a neighbour's dog. It reminded him of other stories, some of which concerned dogs and neighbours, none of which concerned C.P. Michael was relieved when an acned youth arrived to collect the coffee cups.

Daryl, Mr Drew explained, was on work experience and had been given the task of looking out the Hopwood papers, now ready, the youth confirmed with a grunt. He did not give the impression that he had found his true vocation in soliciting.

The first-floor room into which Michael was shown smelled fustily of the books which lined its walls. Outside the window a golden false acacia blocked out most of the daylight. Daryl switched on the light.

'The stuff you want's in them boxes.'

A walnut dining table and one unmatching chair were the only other items of furniture in the room. On the table were two battered cardboard boxes tied with pink ribbon. Huntley and Palmers Biscuits, it said on one of the boxes. Michael approached the table eagerly.

'Money in it, is there? A missing legacy like?'

There was something Dickensian about Daryl, his spare frame, hunched at the shoulders, the quick opportunist eyes. He fidgeted as Michael explained. There had to be money in it. Why else would anyone want to root about in a load of mouldy old papers!

Eventually alone, Michael slung his jacket over the back of the chair. He sat down with the first box in front of him, pulling the pink bow apart slowly, with anticipation, and lifted the lid. On the top of the papers inside was a sketchbook, dog-eared, yellowed with age. He took it out and opened it. Inside were pencil drawings of farm buildings, of timber joints and carved decoration. *Stave Church, Telemark*, the initials *C.P.H.* on every page. It was Hopwood's record of his Norwegian tour. With mounting excitement Michael turned the pages: *Houses in Hallingdal, Viking Artefacts, Oslo.* This was alone was priceless. *Romcke's House, Nesbyen.* He put the sketchbook on one side, reluctantly, and returned to the box. The remaining contents were less exciting; invoices, receipts, a programme for the 1889 Paris Exhibition. There was a buff foolscap folder containing letters received on his tour, never to be looked at again, some from Hopwood's stepfather, rather formal, about allowances, a brief and impersonal note from his mother regarding warm shirts and embrocation, and two in a different and confident masculine hand. He scanned the first one of these.

Half-way down the page he stopped abruptly. A single word had tripped him. He found it again– *chapel*! *Your chapel is completed*!

Slowly he returned to the start of the letter. It was dated August 1898, Birmingham.

My Dear Hoppy,

How good it was to receive your letter. Thoughts of you wandering in the northern wilderness sustain me through the boredom of a humid English summer. While you face bear and elk, I am confronted by worthy Midlanders who growl through their moustaches, like walruses. I am permitted to design the odd factory gate for them, providing, of course, that it is Classical in style. I should like to shock them all with some of this voluptuous Art Nouveau from the Continent; the old fellow would be apoplectic! Do you remember his face when you left?

Your chapel is completed and is a fine thing. I overheard Lord Fairybridge congratulating old Gosplett on it last week; jewel in the crown, he said, jewel in the crown. Gosplett neglected to mention you, of course; just accepted the praise in his usual fawning way. I am sure he would have preferred it to be Greek Revival like the court itself. He is going down to Glostwich for the opening next month. There is talk of the Prince of Wales being there. There is no talk of yours truly attending, though I have been acting as clerk of works. I should tell you I took the opportunity to get Pugh to sign the chapel with your initials. It's only right. Gosplett didn't notice.

I weary of architecture sometimes, despite your kind endorsement of my talent. Perhaps I should join you in the wilderness. I long for adventure, for new horizons. The Empire must need me, to quell a few natives, to find the source of some river. New Zealand, maybe, or the Dark Continent. There is but one reason I remain, and I think you know it: the best, the most beautiful of reasons, my intended – Isabel!

The letter ran to several pages, with no further mention of
the chapel. It ended:

Your truest of friends, James Cranham
    P.S. I am sending this to your forwarding address in
Lillehammer, in the fond hope that a reindeer is due in your
direction shortly.

Michael sat back in his chair. So, there it was, his proof. He
went to see Mr Drew to ask if he could telephone Mrs Hopwood-
Brown. There was a long delay before her cracked voice came on
the line.

'Damned slow, these nurses,' she said crossly, 'must get myself
one of those mobile phones.'

He told her of his find. Would she mind if he borrowed the
letter?

'Borrow the lot,' she said, 'better in the hands of someone
who's interested in them than languishing on a dusty shelf. You
can bring them to me when you've finished with them and take
me out for tea. I believe it's all right for a lady to do the asking
these days.' She asked to speak to Mr Drew.

'You just need to sign for them,' he said on putting the phone
down, 'I must say it will save some valuable space. We have some
books that belong to the family too. I don't suppose you'd like
to take those with you?'

Michael declined. He could imagine what Andrea was going
to say about the junk he was already taking. He would have to
stash the boxes in the garage as it was. He wondered, however,
if the books had been Hopwood's too.

* * *

'Looks pretty convincing to me,' Geoff Lomax said, having read the letter, 'but before we slap a preservation notice on the building we could do with some visual evidence, photographs or drawings.' He took photocopies, however, to send, when the time came, to English Heritage. 'Another couple of decades and we should get the chapel listed.' He grinned. 'Actually, they've speeded up recently. Must be the Government's threat to make them tender for the service against Madame Tussauds and the Disney Corporation.'

Michael was never quite sure when Lomax was serious. He smiled.

He would not have smiled had he been able to eavesdrop on a conversation taking place at the same time in a corner of the Glendower Arms, where Marcus Groat and his financial adviser were lunching.

'Yes,' said the financial adviser, 'your wife's windfall will be invested offshore, in her maiden name of course, quite probably in the Virgin Islands. Should make her a tidy profit over a year or two.' Groat grunted.

'It would be even tidier if she was to sell some more of the Fairybridge estate,' he said, draining the last drops of Nuit St George from his glass. The financial adviser raised his eyebrows.

'Is it not an Area of Outstanding Natural Beauty, Marcus?'

'It was zoned so, but the civic centre sets a precedent. There will be a new two-lane road serving it, with services and drains. That road could be extended into the parkland beyond. The area is screened by woodland on three sides. I'd say we could fit seventy-five to a hundred executive houses on there.' Groat poured himself another glass of wine, 'There's just one problem. That heap of rubble, the planners and that young architect are calling a chapel, is in the way. They're trying to get it listed.' His eyes narrowed. 'That,' he said, 'would be most unfortunate!'

* * *

Michael stopped at the market and took home some flowers for Andrea, forgetting that Wednesday was her night out. Take up a sport, he had suggested to her complaint of boredom. Badminton, he had thought vaguely, they could both do that. Scuba diving would not have been on his list. The club was alongside a flooded quarry in Church Newington, necessitating an early start and a late return. It was a pity, he thought as he forked through his take-away *tikka masala*, that he had never learned to swim.

Andrea's absence, however, afforded an opportunity to browse once more through the Hopwood papers. He brought the first box in from the garage. It was pure luck that the first letter he had read had contained the reference to the chapel. But now he was curious to know more about James Cranham and his friendship with the great man. Pushing aside the foil trays he took out a second letter and began to read.

Birmingham, November 1898

My Dear Hoppy,

I am glad to hear from you and to know you will return to England before the winter sets in. I do not know your subsequent plans, but when I mentioned your situation to my fiancée's family, they insisted that you should join with me in spending Christmas with them at Nether Suckley in Shropshire, where my future father-in-law is rector. They are the kindest of people and will make you most welcome, so I urge you to accept their invitation. If you travel by train, I will borrow the Bensons' trap and meet you at Shrewsbury station.

Perhaps we can do some winter walking together during your stay. The Long Mynd is reasonably close, as are the Stipperstones. I walked on the Malvern Hills recently and was able look down upon Mr Voysey's recent creation, the house called Perrycroft. It is a gem, so modern, and surrounded by what will be gorgeous gardens when they mature. Miss Jekyll, of course! I must tell you that, despite my recent disillusionment with architecture, I have been inspired enough to enter a design competition for a house in the South-West, sponsored by Morris & Co. It seems to be going well, though I must work on it in my lodgings and using my own materials, of course! Old Gosplett counts each week his stock of double elephant sheets against drawings produced! I have, however, found a new paper maker in Bridgnorth who is quite competitive. You must look over my scheme after Christmas and give me your opinion. I look forward with great pleasure to meeting with you again.

Your friend as ever,
James Cranham

Chapter Nine

Aware that Michael was not enthusiastic about the design as it had evolved, Spynk had decided that he would present the scheme to the Central Planning Committee himself. It was not until the morning after, therefore, that Michael was informed of the outcome. Geoff Lomax had come over from the Planning Department and was already ensconced in Spynk's office when Michael was called in.

The good news was that the application had been successful, Lomax informed him. There were, however, conditions. The first was that additional carparking was to be provided for members on the surface, by the front entrance.

Michael gaped.

'But that's the terrace, the view over the lawn to the lake! The ha-ha!'

'Ha-ha indeed! Access for disabled councillors, you see!' Michael recalled the councillors at the meeting he had attended, one walking stick and a speech impediment.

'But there's a lift from the basement, for staff *and* members.'

'Ah, there you have it, my friend. Shared use, smacks of socialism! Can't have that!' Lomax smiled sadly. 'The good news is that you can keep the cedars. Even if you have to drop a couple of car spaces. Wouldn't want to lose the green vote, would we?' There was a minority opinion that we fill in the lake, however.

Health and Safety again. That was dropped for the present, fortunately.'

'And the chapel, what about that?' Lomax glanced at Spynk.

'Well, that's the other condition,' said Spynk, 'if it is listed, then it will be restored and adapted as a council chamber. It was felt, however, that we need further evidence that it is worthy of restoration before recommending to English Heritage that it should be listed. While your evidence that it is the work of Hopwood is convincing, we could benefit from some attributable drawings or photographs, as I understand Mr Lomax has advised you. We have until the next Central Area Planning meeting to find that proof. I am afraid that I cannot allow you carry out research during office hours, but you are free to do so in your own time.'

Geoff Lomax winked conspiratorially as Michael rose to leave.

'Another thing while you're here, Michael,' Spynk said. 'You and your team will be commencing the production drawings as of today. We have appointed a structural engineer to assist you. As we are proposing to utilise the basement of the old court as a carpark, the engineer will need to look at the ground conditions straight away. The Council's solicitor, therefore, has agreed that we can dispense with tenders, allowing us to engage a local contractor to clear all rubble from the basement of Fairybridge Court in the next few weeks. On the chief executive's recommendation, I have agreed,' and here faint distaste crept into his voice, 'that Diggers and Shifters Ltd will do that work. Thank you.'

Michael returned to the drawing office,

'So, we're using Diggers and Shifters, are we?' said Ronnie Barge. 'A right bunch of cowboys, they are!'

* * *

That day, Michael revised the site layout plan. As well as the cedars, he reserved some areas within the carpark for new planting, some late Victorian favourites he suggested to the Council's parks and gardens officer. The plan arrived back a few days later, a frogspawn of circles filling the plant beds. The species included a giant rhubarb, a cultivated bramble and the Rosa Henry Kissinger, a variety, the book said, particularly resistant to exhaust fumes. Michael added a Cappadocian maple. He had never seen one but liked the name.

Disregarding Spynk's instructions, he rang on his office phone the West Midlands branch of the Royal Institute of British Architects and asked its archivist to find out what she could about Henry Gosplett's Birmingham practice. The following afternoon, she rang him back.

Gosplett had died in 1920. The practice had struggled through the Depression under his junior partner, Sidney Small, and was eventually absorbed by the partnership of McKinley and Patterdale (to whose title Small was appended) moving to their office in Coventry. On the fourteenth of November 1940 the office was completely destroyed by a German incendiary bomb. No records survived.

Michael thanked her. The chances of discovering a drawing of the chapel, at best remote, were now zilch. He returned glumly to his board.

* * *

At Fairybridge the rural tranquillity had been broken by the arrival of a fleet of lorries and a large excavator. Work had commenced on the removal of the rubble which had once been the superstructure of the court from its own basement. Michael left his car out of the way on the road and walked down the track, already rutted by the wheels of the lorries, towards the growls of engines and the screech of steel on masonry. Overhanging branches had been torn from trees and left at the side of the track. A silver birch was snapped off at head height. The smell of diesel hung in the air.

As Michael came out of the trees, he spotted Arthur Brickbatt chatting to the Diggers and Shifters foreman, who abruptly returned to the ruins. The clerk of works came to meet him, grinning.

'Good man, that Dave. Used to work with him years ago.'

'That's as maybe, Arthur,' Michael said sternly, adopting the slightly distant attitude he considered appropriate when dealing with artisans, 'but he's allowing his drivers to destroy the environment.' He pointed out the trail of destruction behind himself. Arthur's grin disappeared. He had clearly not noticed.

'Right, I'll have a word with him. Get some protection set up. Apart from that, I think you'll find things are progressing well.' They walked over to the excavations. The digger was perched on the edge of the basement, its bucket scooping up debris, roof slates, scorched timbers, plaster and masonry, and depositing it into the back of a lorry. Another lorry waited its turn, its driver smoking in the cab.

'Haven't found any bodies yet,' said Brickbatt. They watched for some time. A small circular object fell off the bucket, making a metallic clunk as it struck a loose brick on the ground.

'What's that?' Michael said. The foreman, who had joined

them, held up his hand and the digger driver stopped his machine. The foreman picked up the metal object and wiped it on his sleeve. It was an iron flower about four inches across with six petals and a brass centre.

'We've found a few of those,' he said. Michael examined it; he seen something like it before. It was, he was confident, from the wrought iron balustrade of a staircase.

'Can you keep any you find safe?' he asked. 'I might be able to use them.'

* * *

Virginia Groat, lady wife of the grand chancellor and chairman of the district council, was at a loose end. She had visited the alpacas and supervised the young woman who groomed them. She had walked around the garden with her man and given him instructions for pruning the roses. In her capacity as President of the Glostwich and District Women's Institute she and Mrs Carrington-Smythe, the events secretary had finalised on the phone the list of competitions for the year, next month the knitted tea cosy. She felt somehow undervalued. Her husband was out, attending to this Council business or that Pargetters charity. He had not said where. She was not included in his politics. Not that she was at all interested in his grubby little world. Virginia, she had been told repeatedly by her family, had married beneath her. Her great uncle was, after all, the last Lord Fairybridge, aristocrat, friend to royalty. When she met Marcus, she had been available for several seasons and her asset rich family were increasingly short of the readies.

She wandered around from room to room, picking up glass

and china objects, turning them over. Royal Worcester, Delft, Lalique. She felt that she and her family deserved to be recognised in their own right. They were part of the history of Glostwich. On impulse she opened the cupboard where the old Fairybridge family albums were kept, musty and yellowing. Which one was it? She had not looked at them in years. One album looked familiar, she took it into the drawing room and browsed through it. Yes, that was the picture she remembered; quite informal for its time; her great uncle bending to pat his retriever, alongside an ornate fountain. Beside him, also clad in plus-fours, a shotgun broken over his arm, the stout figure and lugubrious features of Edward, Prince of Wales. To their left was the great portico of Fairybridge Court.

Very much in the news, Fairybridge Court, the chosen site for the Council's new civic centre. She picked up the phone, rang the *Glostwich Bugle* and asked for the features editor.

'Virginia Groat here,' she said. 'I have an old photograph here you might find interesting.'

* * *

If the features editor was interested in all matters Fairybridgian, the same could not said of Andrea. In vain did Michael try, over their evening meal, to keep her up to date with developments. Her eyes would glaze perceptibly over, especially if Hopwood entered the conversation.

'Really?' she would say, between mouthfuls of cauliflower cheese, or 'What would you expect?' This of the vagaries of local government decisions, or lack of them. Michael had resolved to show some interest in her own areas of concern.

'So, how's the scuba diving progressing?' he asked.

'Fine,' she said, 'just fine!'

'Only I noticed your wet suit was still on the line the other night after you left for Church Newington.' She gave him a sharp look.

'We don't go in the water every time. It was theory this week, about shipwrecks and – poor visibility.'

'Sounds interesting,' Michael said., 'I might come along one night.'

'Shouldn't bother. You'd probably find it boring.' Andrea resumed her attack on the cauliflower cheese. There was a period of silence.

'We found some wrought iron flowers on site today,' Michael said eventually, 'I'm pretty sure they were from the staircase balustrade.'

* * *

At another dining table in the vicinity, Marcus Groat spluttered into the wine glass he had just raised to his lips. He placed the glass on its coaster.

'You did what?' Virginia was unperturbed.

'Gave a photograph to the *Bugle* showing the Prince of Wales visiting Fairybridge Court, my family home. It's about heritage, but you wouldn't understand that, would you?' Groat reddened.

'You stupid woman! Why don't you keep your aristocratic nose out of things! We're trying to play down the history of the court, not to draw attention to it! Now every irk in the district will know what's happening.'

'And a good thing too!' Virginia shouted after her husband,

who was heading for the phone in the entrance hall. Groat rang the editor's home.

'Frank!' His tone was conciliatory. 'About the photograph my wife gave you. It's a rather delicate matter. How shall I put it? The Prince of Wales wasn't here just for the shooting. You know what he was like! Some family sensibilities involved; his visit has always been kept secret.' The rest of the conversation was indistinct. When Groat came back his expression was baleful. 'Too late, it's gone to press.'

Virginia allowed herself a smile of triumph.

* * *

Two days later, Michael was waiting to pay for his lunchtime tuna and cucumber sandwich in the corner shop near the office, when his attention was drawn to a headline in the *Glostwich Bugle* displayed on an adjacent rack.

ROYAL VISITOR TO FAIRYBRIDGE COURT

He bought a copy and took it back to the office to read with his lunch. The article was sycophantic and as normal for the *Bugle*, inaccurate. A large photograph dominated the front page, depicting, the paper said, *Lord Fairybridge on a shooting weekend with his close friend, the Prince of Wales, soon to be crowned King Edward VI. At Fairybridge Court, the site of the Council's new offices.* The photograph had lost some definition in the enlargement of the central figures, so that the court showed little of its architecture.

Michael finished his sandwich and rang the *Bugle*, asking to speak to Tracy, the reporter he knew who had the unenviable task of sitting in on Council meetings.

'I know, I know, we got the regnal number wrong,' she said.

'It's not that,' Michael assured her, 'I just wondered if you could let me have an unedited version of the photograph. Or could it be copyright or something?'

'I don't see why it should be. After all, it's already spread around the district. Tell you what, I'll drop a copy off for you on my way home tonight. No problem!' she responded to his thanks. Michael, Tracy realised, could be a useful source of inside information at the district council, and besides, she quite fancied him.

* * *

True to her word, an A4 envelope bearing his name was on the receptionist's desk when Michael left that evening. He had been working late on a drainage plan. He took the envelope home with him and settling into an armchair with a can of Guinness, opened it. Andrea had yet to return. It was evident that the picture in the *Bugle* had been substantially cropped. Much more of the portico of Fairybridge Court could be seen in the photograph before him. But behind and to the right of the figures by the fountain, he leapt out of his chair spilling Guinness in all directions, was the chapel, Hopwood's chapel, intact, his signature rose window gracing its gable. It was at this precise moment that Andrea arrived home.

'Yes, that should do it,' said Geoff Lomax next morning 'We'll get it to Central Area Planning and slap a building preservation notice on it. Should be plain sailing from then on. Nicely done, Michael, I admire your tenacity.'

Chapter Ten

With the provenance of the chapel all but established, the working drawings for Fairybridge Court crept steadily forwards, despite a cold war with the structural consultant. There were skirmishes too with the heating engineer who, being rather proud of his pipes, took every opportunity to expose them. Gate valves flowered in the foyer; galvanized cowls sprouted like fungi through the roof. It took all Michael's vigilance to control them. Inevitably some took root.

Because of the tight programme he had to leave Ronnie Barge largely to his own devices. Ronnie's standards, however, were not up to his own.

'No problem,' his assistant assured him as Michael agonised over a tricky balustrade detail, 'just nail a bit of ply on it.' Melamine was another of his favoured materials, that and medium density fibreboard.

Not that either of them fully controlled the detailing any longer, for quantity surveyors were now working on the job, measuring quantities of materials as work proceeded, to save time. This would have been fine, had the quantity surveyors started on the parts of the building already drawn, like the foundations or the drains, but the quantity surveyors had their own logic. They started on the wallpaper and worked down and outwards. As Michael worked on the seating layout for the Council Chamber,

Glostover's in-house QS, Herbert Price, would press him for a decision on the floor finish in the foyer. So that later, when he came to consider the foyer and became convinced that blue brick pavers laid to a herringbone pattern, were the answer, he found that PVC floor tiles had been measured.

'That's what you asked for,' the QS said, 'you can't afford brick pavers anyway.' Michael's heart sank whenever his owl-like features appeared around the office door. It was one of life's ironies that the architect, visionary and optimist, had to work so closely with the ultimate pessimist. Realist, the quantity surveyor would have said. It was not easy to take a sanguine view of life when one was a regular reader of *Spon's Architects' and Builders' Price Book*.

* * *

Feeling somewhat stressed, Michael took a Friday off, this being the Friday that Andrea was gifted at regular intervals to compensate for working weekends. He figured he owed his wife something for the Guinness stains on their white fabric sofa. His suggested visit to a National Trust property, however, went down badly.

'If you think I'm going to trail around some fusty old stately home all day, looking at portraits of long-dead ancestors, you've got another thought coming! Especially if it was designed by your sodding Hopwood bloke.'

'We could have lunch there. They always do some nice soup at those places. And cakes,' he added, knowing her weaknesses. It was indeed a Hopwood house he had had in mind. Andrea's expression was withering.

And so, Michael found himself spending his treasured day off, trailing around Merry Hill shopping centre, riding the escalators, and lugging an ever-expanding collection of clothes bags in the wake of his retail focussed wife. The soup and the cakes in the mall restaurant were passable, but not in Michael's opinion, up to National Trust standards. He found himself looking forward to Monday morning. But not for long!

'What do you mean, you've had to change the window proportions?'

Michael gawped at the drawing on Ronnie Barge's board. A razor blade had been employed on the main civic centre elevations. Instead of a subtle diminution in size from ground floor to first, from first floor to second, the windows had been standardised. All were now the squat shape of those on the second floor, the ghosts of the originals still faintly visible beneath.

'It was the structural engineer. He reckons there was a wind loading problem. Too much glass, not enough wall. I told him you wouldn't like it.' Michael resolved not to take Fridays off in future. He reached for the phone, dialled, and waited impatiently for a response.

'Philip Stein, please.'

'One moment, sir.' The receptionist at P. E. Stein and partners lapsed into whispered Brummie. 'It's that artitett frum the Council.' There was a deal of crackling and two bars of Beethoven's synthesised Sixth, then the engineer's oily voice.

'Michael! And what can I do for you this fine Monday morning?'

'You can tell me why my elevations have been desecrated,' Michael said sternly. Ronnie snorted behind him. The voice on the phone lost its bonhomie. It explained, as a teacher might address a five-year-old, the principles of wind calculations. It quoted Codes of Practice and B.R.S. Digests. It had been prepared for his objections. It lost him.

'But there are hundreds of traditional buildings with more windows than this,' Michael said, 'and they're still standing. Look at – Hardwick Hall!' *Hardwick Hall, more glass than wall,* ran the rhyme. Philip Stein was not familiar with the edifice.

'Elizabeth the First, Derbyshire,' Michael informed him.

'The Tudors didn't have Codes of Practice to contend with,' Stein said.

'But the Tudors did have wind,' Michael said.

'Especially Henry the Eighth,' said Ronnie Barge.

Surely there was another way to achieve the wind resistance. Lateral internal walls, but they would break up the open plan; steel stiffening around the windows.

'But,' said the engineer, 'your boss has already discounted those measures. Dishonest, I think he called it.'

Michael went off to see Maxwell Spynk.

'You sort him out,' Ronnie Barge encouraged him, continuing to scratch out the windows. In ten minutes, Michael was back. 'What did he say?'

'That sufficient daylight for a second-floor office was sufficient for an identical office on the first floor. That the simple approach was often the best, young man.'

'Oh well,' said Ronnie cheerfully, 'but I wouldn't need to do all this scratching out if we had CAD!' For several months Ronnie had been pestering to be sent on a course in Computer Aided Design. Michael resumed work on the chapel's rose window, the Quest for the Holy Grail.

'That's as maybe, Ronnie, but CAD takes out all the individuality from architecture. We'd all be robots.'

'That would be good for dealing with councillors, said Ronnie, waving his razor-blade in the air. 'Exterminate the Groat, he commanded the vertical filing cabinet in the corner of the drawing office. 'Exterminate, exterminate!

Wednesday came around again. Before leaving for her evening class, Andrea had left a note on the kitchen worktop:

> The hinges on the crockery cupboard need adjusting. The right-hand door won't close properly. In fact, all the doors need adjusting. Back about 10.00 pm.
>
> Andrea x

Michael opened the right-hand door of the crockery cupboard. It was indeed askew. He shrugged and took out a dish into which he emptied a tin of mulligatawny soup. While it microwaved, he found a heel of bread which he toasted, consuming the resultant meal in front of the early evening television news. Then he went into the garage for a screwdriver. He was about to return to the house when the two cardboard boxes from the Shrewsbury solicitor caught his attention. He had taken a quick look previously at the second box and dismissed it, the contents appearing to be just odds and ends belonging to Hopwood's wife, Eleanor, recipes, seating plans for dinner parties and the like. Nevertheless, he picked up the box and carried it into the house. The screwdriver remained on the bench.

At the bottom of the box were several exercise books. These proved to be Mrs Hopwood's diaries, or more accurately, those of Eleanor Benson, written before her marriage to the great man. Michael was curious but felt a little uneasy about reading them. How would Dora Hopwood-Brown feel, exposing her mother's private thoughts to a stranger. But, he reasoned, the old lady had no idea that the diaries existed. What the eye does not see, the heart does not grieve about. He settled into the sofa and began to read.

Most of the entries were quite domestic in tone, concerning Eleanor's gentile life as the daughter of a country rector, harvest festivals and village fêtes, new dresses and picnics in the Shropshire hills. There were many gaps in the narrative, reflecting, perhaps, the similarity of any one day's happenings to the next. One entry, however, caught Michael's eye. There were names in it which he recognised. He went back to its beginning.

20 December 1898

How I look forward to Christmas this year! It has been confirmed that Isabel's fiancée, James, will be joining us at Nether Suckley for the holiday. My sister is so happy. She dances around the house like a fairy princess and sings the old carols like an angel. Sometimes I envy her – we are so different! She is fair and I am dark, I am quiet, and she is full of life. And James is so handsome, a little mischievous, inclined to tease, but I know he is a good man and will take care of her. He brings with him a friend, a Mr Hopwood, who has no close family and who has lately returned from the wilds of Norway. Father insisted that he join us – no man should spend Christmas alone, he says. I hope he will not find us plain and uninteresting after his recent experiences. And here I must cease writing to complete the wrapping of my presents.

The next entry was dated a week later.

28 December 1898

It was indeed a most wonderful Christmas! Our guests arrived on the afternoon of the Eve, though James had come earlier and taken the trap to collect his friend from Shrewsbury station. After dinner the six of us sat by a blazing fire and told each other seasonal stories. Father read Dickens aloud to us, as is his habit, and Isabel played the piano, some pieces by an Edward Elgar, who is I believe an organist in Worcester. James had anecdotes, no doubt embellished, about pompous clients falling into snowdrifts and the like, and I recited a poem by Christina Rossetti. Father disapproves of the Rossettis and their friends, but even he had to admit the poem's beauty. And Mr Hopwood spoke of the fiords and forests of Scandinavia, its Viking art and folklore. He has brought us all gifts from his travels. Mine, which I shall cherish always, is a small female figure carved from the tusk of a walrus.

Late in the evening we all wrapped ourselves in cloaks and scarves and walked across the winter garden, through the churchyard gate, and to the church for midnight mass, Father and Mother, James and Isabel, and myself bringing up the rear on the arm of Mr Hopwood. The church was full, the villagers sang with gusto, and Father's sermon was, thankfully, short but very sweet.

Christmas Day itself was, of necessity for the family of a rector, very full, with two more services, morning and evening. In between them we enjoyed a large and satisfying lunch, for which we gave thanks to God, and to Mrs Merry, our cook. There was sufficient left for we younger folk to take out to the poorer families of the village.

On Boxing Day, the four of us, well wrapped again, took out the carriage with old Moses in the shafts as far as Church Stretton, where we left him with a livery stable and proceeded on foot up

Carding Mill Valley onto the Long Mynd. James had drawn a beautiful map of our route, and Mr Hopwood set the pace, being well accustomed to the outdoor life, though he always slowed to assist me over stiles and such obstacles. It was a beautiful cold winter's day, so clear that we were able to follow the progress of the Hunt in the valley below. It was nearly dark by the time we got back to Nether Suckley, tired but happy.

Yesterday our guests departed. The house seems so quiet without them, both of them. Father seems most impressed with Mr Hopwood, he likes his authoritative bearing, the way he holds one's gaze in conversation. I am a little surprised that Isabel, not known for her reticence, averts her eyes when he addresses her. For my part, I would be disappointed if Christmas 1898 was the last occasion on which Mr Hopwood paid us a visit at Nether Suckley.

She ended the entry on a patriotic note.

The last year of the nineteenth century approaches. Pray God that the Queen lives to see us through it and into a new era of peace and prosperity.

The map which James had drawn was pinned to the sheet. It was indeed beautiful with graphic architectural lettering and a north point in the shape of a stylised bird of prey, its outstretched wings representing east and west and the letter N cleverly incorporated into its head.

So, this was the first meeting of Hopwood with his future bride. Michael returned the diary to its box. There was something he was supposed to be doing before Andrea's return. An idea, however, was beginning to form in his head. Hopwood's later life was well documented in several biographies, one such on his own bookshelves, but here was a new source of information, not previously available to the architectural press. Before Michael had chosen his profession, he had harboured a fancy for the written word. Was this the time to combine his interests and embark on a biography himself? Thoughtfully he carried the box back into the garage, where the screwdriver caught his eye. Oh yes, the kitchen cabinets. Tools in hand he returned to his task, which proved oddly satisfying. By the time he had finished all the door edges were parallel, the gaps around them even. He stood back and admired his work. Sometimes he wished that he had a simple creative manual job, yet here he was running a complex architectural project, and contemplating a new academic career as an author. He smiled ruefully.

He would, of course, need Mrs Hopwood-Brown's permission to use her mother's diaries as a basis for his biography. For a moment he thought about writing her a letter, then he remembered what she had said to him on the phone. He would give her a ring and take her out for tea.

It was 10.30 pm when Andrea came home. After inspecting the kitchen cabinets, she yawned several times and went up to bed. By the time Michael had locked up and brushed his teeth, she was asleep and gently snoring, as she did most nights, though always denying it in the morning. He leant on one elbow and watched her affectionately for a while, before turning off the bedside light. He dreamt that night that he was driving a trap through the Shropshire countryside, a horse called Moses in front and Andrea sitting at his side, resplendent in a full-length dress with ruffles at her throat and an enormously wide brimmed hat.

Chapter Eleven

Diggers and Shifters' excavation of the cellar of Fairybridge Court had not revealed any problems with ground conditions. The proposed basement was still above the water table, despite the proximity of the silted-up lake. Philip Stein, the structural engineer, was satisfied that the whole civic centre could be safely built off a thick reinforced floor slab with standard tanking to the basement walls. This was fortunately what the quantity surveyor had already measured. Michael was thus able to instruct Diggers and Shifters to tidy up the site and remove the remaining mechanical plant. Despite Ronnie Barge's labelling of them as cowboys, it appeared that the ground workers had done a reasonably good job.

The Working Drawings and Bills of Quantities were complete. It was time to invite tenders for the construction work, a process to which Michael was happily not privy. As usual one major regional contractor was to be included together with several local builders from the approved list. Those not selected demanded to know why and put pressure on their councillors to give them a chance. A series of such members entered Maxwell Spynk's office and left angrily stating they would be taking the matter further with the chief executive. Eventually a list of six firms was approved by the Policy and Finance Committee, the dissatisfied compensated with promises of future inclusion.

In the hell-like basement of the Technical Services Department, the taciturn Albert Grimshaw, two years over retirement age, spent a whole day feeding the negative drawings into a medieval dyeline print machine and folding the six resultant copies of each in the prescribed manner so that the title box in the bottom right-hand corner was always displayed. It was said he had never had a cold, no germ being able to survive the ammonia charged atmosphere of the print room. To save time and postage each tenderer collected their heavy bundle of drawings and bills from reception, hoping as they did so to be able to spot and identify who they were up against. There followed, what should have been, a six-week period of relative calm in Michael's office.

It was a good time to take some leave. Michael drove out to the Wyebrae nursing home, having the previous day rung the matron and arranged a date with Dora Hopwood-Brown. She was waiting impatiently in the lounge when he arrived. Other residents looked on blankly as, with the help of the staff, he manoeuvred the old lady out to his car, established her in the passenger seat and stowed the folding wheelchair in the boot.

'Make sure you stop at a place with a disabled toilet,' one of the nurses said to Michael behind her hand. He nodded, having already sussed out several pubs and restaurants on the phone.

'What was that tart whispering about?' Dora asked as they drove off. He told her. There was no point in prevaricating with Mrs Hopwood-Brown.

'But before we have lunch, I thought you might like a little tour around the area.' The Upper Wye Valley was bathed in warm sunshine.

'That would be very nice,' she said, 'and I can bore you with my local knowledge as we go. Drive on, McDuff!'

They crossed the river on Bredwardine bridge, close by the vicarage where the diarist, Francis Kilvert, had lived, a little too fond, according to Dora, of adolescent girls. Passing Clifford Castle, she was reminded of the Fair Rosamunde, long term mistress of King Henry the Second.

'She must have been hot stuff,' Dora said. 'It was a long royal ride from London.' They drove over the invisible border into Wales, and up towards Gospel Pass at the northern end of the Black Mountains, where Michael parked on the long grassy level overlooking Hay-on-Wye. He wound down the window to let in the moorland air, glancing sideways at his passenger, eagerly picking out features in the panorama below them. The daughter of Charles Pericles Hopwood, here in his car! He felt humble.

'I used to walk around here in my youth. That lump,' Dora said, gesturing towards the mountain on their left, 'is Twmpa in Welsh, but the English call it Lord Hereford's Knob. An inappropriate name, I always felt, and somewhat flattering.' They sat for a while, absorbing the view, the scents of grass and bracken, the flight of a bird of prey that Dora identified as a red kite. Then Michael looked at his watch.

'We'd better go. I booked a table for 12.30 at a restaurant in Hay.' He reversed the car and set off back down the road on which they had come. 'I hope you like it.' He need not have worried.

For a woman of her years, Dora did considerable justice to a mushroom omelette and salad, following it up with a generous slice of cheesecake. She even enjoyed a small glass of white wine. The restaurant was, as promised, wheelchair friendly, and when they arrived the female proprietor had taken her straight to the disabled toilet and waited outside for her. As the coffee was served, Dora sat back in her chair and eyed Michael quizzically.

'Right,' she said, 'much as I appreciate being wined and dined, and ferried about the countryside by a charming young man, I am aware that you wish to ask me something, presumably about Papa.' Michael smiled sheepishly. Then he told her about his discovery of her mother's diaries, that he was considering writing a biography of her father, that he needed her permission to take things further.

'And what scandals have you unearthed so far, Mister Maby?'

'None at all,' he reassured her, 'the diaries are just about how your mother met Mr Hopwood, and her quiet life in Nether Suckley Rectory with your grandparents and her sister, Isabel.'

'Aunt Isabel! She was a suffragette, you know, never married.'

'But she was betrothed, was she not?' Michael was shocked.

'I believe her fiancée died abroad, somewhere in Africa; I think. It was never talked about. And we saw very little of Aunt Isabel. She didn't get on with my father. I don't know why. It's a shame because I always admired her. As for my grandparents, I hardly remember them. I was very much the youngest child, the mistake you might say, and grandparents didn't live so long in those days. I vaguely recall their kindness but little else. Family history doesn't interest me a great deal, Michael. When you don't have anyone to pass it on to, there's little point to knowing about your ancestors.' She looked sad for a moment.

'You go ahead and write your book, Michael. I sense you are at a crossroads in your career. I went through it too. We start off as artists, don't we? Writers can write what they like, painters can paint what they like. As an architect there's no such freedom, too many factors involved, money, politics, crooks. But don't let the bastards grind you down!' She grinned and drained her coffee cup.

'Right, you can take me home now. And on the way you can tell me more about your beautiful wife. What's all this about scuba diving?'

* * *

On the way back from the nursing home, Michael had to pass the gate to Fairybridge Court, which was open. Though he was on leave, he could not resist the temptation to see what was going on. He turned onto the track. On the first bend he had to pull over to allow a lorry loaded with spoil to pass him. Reaching the court itself he saw that just the site agent together with one digger and its driver remained. The site agent did a double take.

'Arthur said you were taking a day off, Mr Maby.' Michael smiled.

'I can't keep away,' he said, 'I thought you'd be out of here by now.'

'The last lorry load has just gone. You probably saw it. We're just tidying up and parking the digger for the night. The flat bed will be here tomorrow to collect it. It was needed on another site this afternoon.'

'That's fine. Just ignore me. I'll have a look around by myself.' Michael strolled over to the excavation, the vast flat-bottomed pit which had once been the cellar of Fairybridge Court, now devoid of all its rubble. He walked around it, admiring the precise way in which the banks had been cut in readiness for the new building, then continued down towards the shell of the chapel on its knoll. The two contractor's men were hanging about, probably, he thought, thwarted in their plans for an early finish.

'Don't wait for me,' Michael shouted across the site. 'I'll lock the gate when I leave.' He wandered into the chapel and looked around him, at the floor now cleared of debris, the commodious space revealed. Outside, with metallic clangs and the revving of engines, the digger was parked up for the night. Despite the absence of a roof, Michael noted, the thick walls of the chapel were repelling much of the cacophony. With a roof, and the absorbent finishes and soft furnishings he had specified, he was confident that the acoustics of the Council Chamber would be fine. He stood at one end of the space, with his back to what would be the rose window and delivered a silent speech to the jackdaws perched on the opposite gable.

'And finally, Mr Chairman, I propose that the entire Architects' Section should receive a two hundred per cent increase in salary!' There was a roar of approval. 'Not including Mr Spynk!' he added. He left the building just in time to see the site agent's car disappearing into the trees. After taking some *before* photographs of the chapel and the hole in the ground, he followed.

* * *

It was only four-thirty when he arrived home. Andrea would be some time. He made himself a cup of tea and settled into the sofa with Eleanor Benson's diaries beside him. He felt much happier reading them now, having received her daughter's approval, especially as the entries were becoming more personal, more revealing. For instance:

Sunday, 5 February 1899

James came to visit yesterday, as he does most weekends. The gaps between seem interminable to my sister but he has a living to make. He is still working for Mr Gosplett but spending his evenings in his lodgings on some project of his own. I fear he is burning the candle at both ends. Mr Hopwood has rooms in the same premises.

James says that he has an allowance from an elderly stepfather, somewhere in the North, but so far has not found any employment worthy of his talents since returning from Scandinavia. He is a proud man and needs to be able to support himself, and my sister. Papa keeps encouraging James to bring him here on his visits. I, perforce, cannot comment!

26 February 1899

Papa's entreaties have succeeded! This weekend James brought his friend to visit us again. There was a light fall of snow which prevented us venturing out in the trap this time, so we stayed indoors and played bridge most of the time. Isabel tells me that Mr Hopwood has been introduced by a cousin to a society of some sort, called the Targetters I think, which he is hoping will provide some architectural work for him. James, she says, does not approve for some reason. Is the society connected with archery, perhaps?

19 March 1899

Mr Hopwood came to visit us today, for the second time this month! And this time he came alone! James was too busy with his architectural project to accompany his friend today. Isabel is, of course, very disappointed. She and Mama took it in turns to chaperone us, which is quite frustrating as it prohibits any intimacies between Mr Hopwood, Charles, and myself. And if truth be told, when Isabel is in the room, Charles's attention is not always directed at me! We did, however, venture unaccompanied into the garden together. I just had to show him the daffodils. And in the shrubbery, out of sight from the house, he kissed me!

23 April 1899

Oh, joy! I was reading in the summer house when Charles arrived yesterday. Isabel made to come for me, but no! He wanted to see Papa and was shown into his study. So, she ran to tell me, and we sat holding hands until Papa came out of his French window and called me in. Charles had left the room. My father had on his stern ecclesiastical look. 'Mr Hopwood,' he said, 'has asked for your hand in marriage. Is it your wish that I give my consent?' I pretended doubt, but the smile breaking out on my face gave me away. 'Yes, oh yes, Papa!' I said. His face softened, there was a tear in the corner of his eye. 'Then I consent with all my heart and wish you every happiness.'

I was sent to the drawing room where Charles awaited, standing with his back to the fireplace. He went down on one knee and asked me to marry him. His face, I have to say, showed no concern that I would answer in the negative, and he had been confident enough to have a large piece of amber which he had brought back from Norway set in diamonds for my ring. It is beautiful. Then the family came in. Having had a few minutes to think about it, Papa saw fit to add a condition to his approval. The wedding, he told Charles, should be postponed until he had secured a regular source of income. But he and Mama too are visibly happy for me. Only Isabel has reservations. This morning in my room she looked into my eyes and asked me if I was sure about Charles. I confess I was cross.

'Of course, I'm sure,' I snapped, 'what gives you cause to doubt it?'

'It's just that there's something about him which frightens me,' she said, 'something I cannot put my finger on.'

'What nonsense,' I said, 'he is just a man, and men are naturally stronger and more powerful than we women, a trait we have to accept!'

'Do we?' she asked. 'Or do men have too much power? Should we not be taking some for ourselves?' She shrugged. 'But we stray from the point, sister. I only have your welfare at heart.'

'My welfare is not in jeopardy,' I said, perhaps a little too coldly. I sometimes worry about Isabel. I see the pamphlets she reads, the meetings she attends in Shrewsbury. She is falling under the influence of those radical women who seek emancipation, suffragettes as I believe they are known.

Michael heard a car on the drive. He dropped the diaries back in the box, the box behind the arm of the sofa. When Andrea came in, he was peeling carrots in the kitchen. She gave him a perfunctory kiss. How was his hot date with Dora, she asked slyly? Michael laughed. He was, however, slightly discomfited and his ears were unaccountably burning. At that very moment, his name was being uttered in the spacious hallway of Groat Hall.

'So, you weren't able to do it? That young man,' Marcus Groat spluttered into the telephone, 'is becoming a liability. Something needs to be done about him!'

Chapter Twelve

The following morning being Saturday, Andrea had a lie-in and Michael returned with a coffee to the diaries. He did not have to read very far before he came to a momentous entry.

7 May 1899

Yesterday morning early, our part-time groom, Will, drove Isabel to Shrewsbury to catch a train into Birmingham for one of her rallies. Our parents were not happy about it, but Isabel can be wilful. She expressed an intention to call on James after the rally to return, she said, a scarf he had lent her on their previous meeting. Why that would not wait until his next visit is uncertain! However, she came back last night in an agitated state, with the scarf still in her handbag. She refused to divulge the reason for her anguish. No, she told me, it was nothing to do with the rally, which had been well attended and peaceful, despite the usual cat calls and lewd gestures from uncouth men along the route. But she now knew that all men, from all stations in life, were the enemy, adding darkly that I too should be aware of that fact! She would not expand on this. And this morning she has written a letter to James breaking off their engagement! This I cannot understand, for I know how much she loves him. It is a matter of honour she insists.

9 May 1899

James arrived at midday unannounced. He was pale and unshaven, with unmatching shirt and tie, brown shoes and a dark grey suit. Isabel saw him through the window and ran upstairs, locking herself in her room. She refused to come out and see him. The poor fellow was distraught. I prevailed on him to come and sit with me in the drawing room, to tell me what had happened two days ago in Birmingham. He was as much at a loss as I was. Evidently, he had not seen Isabel that day, having been persuaded to put in some extra work for old Gosplett. He had not even been aware that she was in town, though he had glimpsed the suffragettes' march passing the end of the street from his office window. My parents joined us; both were visibly upset. I left them and went to talk to Isabel through her door but still she would not see him. We promised James we would attempt to persuade my sister to reconsider her decision, but as Papa said, once Isabel had decided something, she rarely changed her mind, and eventually James rose to leave. When I offered to return his scarf, he had to fight back the tears. He shook his head and left abruptly.

Here Michael was startled by the ringing of the phone. He picked it up.

'Glostwich 563—' he began.

'Michael,' he was interrupted, 'I have some bad news for you.' It was Geoff Lomax. 'It's about your chapel. Can you meet me on site in fifteen minutes? Good man! See you there.' Michael left a hurried note for Andrea and drove out to Fairybridge.

As he approached the site, Michael saw Lomax was already there, talking to the site agent, Dave. He pulled up alongside them and scrambled out of his car. A grim sight met his eyes. On the knoll, where the chapel had been, was a large heap of rubble. A small section of the back wall, about a metre high, was all that remained standing. In front of the ruin, its bucket arm extended into the heap, was the excavator he had seen the day before.

'Oh, my God,' he exclaimed, 'what on earth happened?'

The site agent, looking sheepish, began again the tale he had been telling Lomax.

'Well, me and the digger driver got here early to find the flat bed waiting for us.' He indicated the lorry behind them, its driver eating his sandwiches in the cab. 'So, Pat, that's the digger driver, got on his machine and started it up. I had my back to him and giving Barry, the lorry driver, instructions, when Barry spotted there was something wrong. The digger had left the level area and was moving down the slope towards the lake. We both waved our arms and shouted but Pat was slumped over the wheel. It picked up speed then and veered over to the right. It would have stopped when the caterpillar track hit the knoll, but the arm was fully extended. The bucket smashed into the porch, which was sticking out, and took out the whole of the front wall. Then, without the lateral support, both the gables fell inwards. There's no more than a couple of masonry courses left on top of each other. The building's a complete write-off!'

There was silence as Michael and Geoff Lomax took in the gravity of the situation. Someone had to ask, so Michael did, though it was not his priority at that very moment,

'Was the driver alright?'

'Well, he was unconscious, but we thought it best not to move him. I had a mobile phone in the car.' He waved a black brick sized object in the air, 'So I called an ambulance and we checked him over for any obvious damage. By the time the paramedics arrived he was coming around, and they managed to walk him to the ambulance. They reckoned he'd had a blackout.'

Michael and Lomax exchanged looks.

'I think,' said Lomax, 'that you had better call the police too!' The site agent looked startled. 'And your lorry driver will be required as a witness.' The two of them walked down to the remains of the chapel, as Dave went to inform Barry that his Saturday morning had gone down the chute. Close to the devastation was complete. It looked like a bomb site. Michael stopped to pick up a small fragment of the lattice patterned porch columns.

'At least the chapel had a Building Preservation Notice on it,' he said.

Lomax closed his eyes and shook his head.

'As soon as we had sorted out the provenance, I drafted out a Building Preservation Notice and ran it past the solicitor. However, before we applied to English Heritage for full listing, the chief executive wanted to see the document. I sent it to him. To date he has not responded. I am sorry, Michael. The chapel was not protected!' Michael was aghast.

'So, what are the chances of us getting it listed now?' he asked.

'Very small, I would think,' said Lomax. 'What we have is a pile of rubble. A pile of Neolithic rubble would be one thing, a pile of late nineteenth century rubble another. It was marginal yesterday, But now! The best we can hope for is some compensation from the contractor's insurance, which will not take account of the chapel's architectural or historic value. Hardly an act of God, you would think!'

'And what if it was not an accident?' Michael said. Lomax grimaced.

'I should be very careful what I said about that, Michael, if I was you! They have two witnesses, and nothing to gain from the chapel's destruction.'

They walked back in silence to the vehicles, as a police car arrived with blue light flashing. A bored constable emerged, notebook in hand and took laborious statements from Dave, Barry, and the two representatives of the Council. It was almost lunchtime when Michael got home. He sat for some time on the drive, brooding over what he took to be his personal loss. Rebuilding the whole chapel in the style of Hopwood would be completely uneconomical. Spynk would want to build a new Council Chamber close to the main block, as he had advocated all along. The contractor had *nothing to gain from the chapel's destruction*. So, who had? He could think of several people.

He let himself into the house and wandered disconsolately into the kitchen. On the bottom of the note, he had left for Andrea, she had penned a reply:

Have gone to Birmingham with Julie to a matinee concert. Forgot to tell you about it. Hope all was well on your site.

Andrea x

P.S. There's a pork pie in the fridge.

He ate half of the pie and a wrinkled tomato in the lounge, before picking up the diary he'd been reading before Lomax rang. If he was hoping that Eleanor Benson, as was, had some better news to impart, he was to be disappointed.

* * *

15 May 1899

Isabel has hardly spoken a word all week. She makes an appearance at mealtimes, eats very little, then retires to her room. We are all very concerned about her, she will not explain her actions. I therefore took a train to Birmingham, determined to shed some light on this awful situation. Imagine my frustration when I found that James was not in. I had not heard anything from Charles either since the events of last week so, of course, I then knocked on his door. He was very surprised, and somewhat discomfited, I have to say, by my arrival on his threshold, but he stood back to let me in and attempted to calm me. His news, however, was dreadful. James has resigned his post with Mr Gosplett, terminated his tenancy of the apartment from the end of the month, and has by now left the country for South Africa, an area where Charles says that trouble is brewing again. I know little of the geography but, he tells me, the two Boer republics, buoyed by their success against us twenty years ago, are threatening the border of the Cape Colony. James, he says, is heedless of the danger in which he is putting himself. Charles holds the key for the apartment and has been charged with the disposing of James's meagre belongings. I returned to Nether Suckley, much troubled, and imparted my information to Isabel, who turned deathly pale and broke down. What have I done, Eleanor, she cried, what have I done?

Michael closed the diary. There was just so much depressing news he could take in in one day. He turned on the radio to discover that the Villa, whom he in principle supported, were three-nil down after an early kick-off.

* * *

Over the weekend, Michael resolved to take his mind off the disaster by focussing on research for his biography. Through Eleanor Benson's diaries, he was learning much about Charles Hopwood's early years, but he needed to learn more about his actual architecture. The first building which could be attributed to C.P. was a heap of rubble, though he had photographs of the shell and a blurred image in the background of the Prince of Wales picture. So where could he go next? The earliest building referred to in the coffee table book was a house in Somerset, dating from the turn of the twentieth century, but there were no photographs and little information on it. Perhaps, the RIBA library could help.

* * *

The following Tuesday morning, therefore, saw Michael disembarking from the train at Paddington Station. He had extended his leave by ringing the office the previous day, feeling unable to face the aftermath of the chapel's destruction, and made a call to the RIBA who rang him back with some good news. 'Yes, they had the drawings for Ladysmith House, near Taunton, C. P. Hopwood's first recorded commission.' It had taken a while to find them, however. 'When would he like to see them?'

He took the tube to Regents Park and walked down Portland Place to number sixty-six. It was just a few months since his last visit.

The receptionist watched as he signed in.

'Always good to see members—'

'From the provinces,' he finished the phrase for her. He had thought that he was looking cool this time, in his black leather jacket and white crew-necked sweater. She rang the library and an attractive but severe young lady in a short skirt came to collect him. He attempted conversation as he followed her up the staircase, trying not to look at her bottom, but she was not familiar with Glostwich. 'Was it somewhere near Reading?' she asked politely.

He was allocated a space on a long polished table. There were six or seven other studious looking researchers, one of whom on the other end of his table, examined Michael over his glasses and murmured good morning. He took off his jacket and hung it over the back of the chair while the librarian went out of the room, reappearing shortly struggling with a double-elephant portfolio which she dropped on the table in front of him. She also brought a pair of thin white cotton gloves and watched until he had donned them, before returning to her desk. Michael read the label on the cover of the portfolio.

> Charles Pericles Hopwood. Winning Competition Drawings, Ladysmith House, Taunton, Somerset, for Morris & Co.
> 1 number sheet site plan, scale 1/16 of an inch to 1 foot
> 3 number sheets floor plans, scale ¼ of an inch to 1 foot
> 2 number sheets elevations, scale ¼ of an inch to 1 foot
> 1 number sheet perspective

He lovingly untied the ribbons holding the portfolio together and folded back the front cover. He gasped. While familiar, of course, with photographs of Hopwood's drawings, he had never seen an original. They were exquisite, the draftsmanship superb. The ink had slightly faded but that added to their character.

It was the design of the building itself, however, which was most impressive. The floor plans were spacious and functional, the rooms relating to each other informally, ignoring symmetry but relating to views and purpose and sunshine. The two-storey hall was more than an entrance and intended as a space for family and friends to gather by a huge fireplace, a winding staircase rising casually to a gallery, off which four or five bedrooms opened. Outside a steep slate roof overhung a white stucco wall with long horizontal windows sub-divided by slender mullions into three, five or even seven vertical lights, again ignoring symmetry. A tall tapering chimney pierced the roof above the hall fireplace.

The lettering was innovative and stylish. Michael was envious, used as he was to stencils and Letraset. Text would be even less personal if CAD ever took a hold. Being a competition entry, there was no mention of C. P. Hopwood's name on the drawings, the rules would have required anonymity.

Looking at the site plan Michael could see that the house was at the head of a valley, the major rooms arranged as to take advantage of the view, no doubt facing south. He scanned the drawing for a north point to confirm his guess. It was located, as was the norm, in a corner of the sheet outside the boundaries of the site. It took the form of a bird of prey, its head indicating north, its outstretched wings east and west, the exact symbol that James Cranham had drawn on his Boxing Day route map of the Shropshire Hills. North points had often been used by architects to express their personalities, as signatures even. This one was unique.

Michael sat motionless for several minutes. Then he lifted the site plan, turned it over and held it to the light. The librarian looked up in alarm. There was a watermark on the back of the sheet. *Carberry and Son, Paper Makers, Bridgnorth.* Bridgnorth, where James had discovered a source of reasonably priced drawing paper. And what was James doing that prevented him from visiting his fiancée but working on a competition for a house in the West Country, in his own time, in his rooms in Birmingham, next to rooms occupied by his friend, a friend entrusted with a key.

There was little doubt in Michael's mind. Charles Pericles Hopwood was a plagiarist, a charlatan who had stolen the design, and even the drawings, of his best friend after James had left England for the perils of South Africa, on the eve of the Boer War. Who, very probably, had attempted to seduce his best friend's fiancée, his own fiancée's sister! Michael waited until the librarian was distracted, then standing, took a photograph of the site plan. He replaced all the drawings neatly in the portfolio, tied the ribbons and laid the gloves alongside. Then, with an acknowledging wave to the librarian, he left. He walked all the way back to Paddington.

* * *

In Michael's absence, things had been happening at the office. Spynk had contacted all the tenderers for the civic centre and asked them to omit the whole section dealing with the chapel, comparatively easy to do as it had always been dealt with as a separate entity. After an emergency meeting of the chief officers, it had been decided to abandon the knoll and build an entirely new Council Chamber attached to the main building, as Michael had anticipated. Citing Michael's emotional attachment to the original design, Spynk had opted to design the Chamber himself. And following a meeting with the chief executive, it had been decided that a more experienced architect would be appointed to supervise the contract on site.

Michael took the gypsy site drawings out of the vertical filing cabinet where they had been languishing for the last few months. 'Never mind,' said Ronnie Barge, 'you could be on the streets.' That, thought Michael, was next on the agenda! He picked up his pen. Surely, nothing else could go wrong that week.

* * *

Halfway along Falklands Drive on his way home, Michael's car spluttered to a halt. He glanced at the dashboard to see the fuel gauge needle pointing to empty. The emergency one-gallon petrol can, usually in the boot, was missing. He remembered that Andrea had taken it and used the fuel in her car the previous week. It was a long way on foot to the nearest filling station anyway. He locked the car and walked the remaining quarter of a mile home. Andrea's car was not on the drive. *Oh God, it was Wednesday. She was on her scuba diving course.* He felt a headache coming on. He made a cup of tea and searched the medicine cupboard in vain for a paracetamol.

Just relax, he told himself, all will be well. There was a late opening filling station, he recalled, on the way back from Church Newington. He would ring the Scuba Diving centre and leave a message for Andrea to call at the station and purchase a can of petrol and some paracetamols. He drank his tea and found the number in Yellow Pages. The receptionist responded promptly. How could she help him?

'My name is Maby,' he said, 'I'd like to leave a message for my wife, Andrea, who is on your course tonight.'

'Just one moment, sir.' The receptionist consulted her list. 'I'm sorry, Mr Maby, but your wife hasn't signed in this evening.' 'Are you sure?' Michael was puzzled. She was sure. 'Well, sorry to bother you,' he said. 'Goodbye.' He rang the clinic where Andrea worked. No, Mrs Maby had left at the usual time, said she was going swimming or something. Was there a problem? He assured them all was fine.

So, where was she? It wasn't very likely, but Jane and Oliver lived in Church Newington. Maybe she had called in to see them before the class and stayed too long. They hadn't been in contact since the Ladies' Evening, and he rang their number with some trepidation. Jane answered his call.

'Michael!' To his relief she sounded as warm as ever, 'How are you both?' Both, he noted, so Andrea was evidently not with her. He tried to play down his concern. He was just ringing on the off chance.

'She's probably gone off somewhere on an impulse,' Jane suggested, 'you know what she's like. She'll turn up and wonder what all the fuss was about.' They chatted about inconsequences. It was Michael and Andrea's turn to come to them next time. They would have to make it soon.

'I'm a grass widow tonight too,' said Jane, 'Wednesday is Oliver's military history class. I had no idea he was interested in that sort of thing. But off he goes every Wednesday. I expect he'll find something else soon, like he always does!'

Michael switched the television on. He watched a programme about a random group of people who were trying to make a community on a remote Scottish Island. They had been chosen by the programme makers for their potential to fall out with each other. It kept his mind off Andrea, however. At a quarter past ten, her car pulled onto the drive and Andrea walked in, her hair, as usual on a Wednesday evening, showing signs of immersion. She took her kit out of her bag and hung it to dry on the clotheshorse in the kitchen.

'They had us doing lifesaving and resuscitation tonight,' she said, dropping onto the sofa opposite Michael. He looked at her impassively.

'I expect Oliver's very good at that,' he said. 'The kiss of life and so on. And taking a shower afterwards –now that's a clever touch!'

Chapter Thirteen

Time hung heavily on Michael's shoulders. He had taken to walking by himself in the countryside around Glostwich, armed with binoculars and an Ordnance Survey Explorer map, 2.5 inches to the mile, or 1:25,000 as he personally preferred. His was the generation who had been taught the logical metric system, who used it naturally at school and in the office, and who were now in limbo following the Thatcher government's abandonment of foreign units of measurement. Now you had to fit imperial sized timber windows into metric brick sized openings, to buy carpet by the metre length in yard widths, as he and Andrea had done in recent years. Not that they would be doing that in the future.

They were still occupying number twenty-four, Goose Green, as two individuals. Michael kept the master bedroom with its en-suite, Andrea having the second bedroom and family bathroom. They met intermittently but not socially in the lounge and kitchen, preferring to retire to their rooms to eat their basic meals. Cauliflower cheese figured less in Michael's diet, pizzas and Chinese takeaways more. There were rules. Michael continued to pay the mortgage repayments, while Andrea took over the monthly fuel bills. It was noticeable how lights were now switched off, and washing was hung outside to dry. And the presence of Oliver within sight or hearing of the house was strictly taboo, Andrea having to walk around the corner onto

Falklands Drive to be picked up several times a week, in the silver-green Corvette Coupé. From what Michael had learned, a similar regime was in operation in Church Newington. He had rung Jane the morning after the night class disclosure and was taken aback by the calm way she received the news. It was almost as if she was expecting it. Since then, however, there had been tears and retribution pouring from the telephone. The thought had entered his mind unbidden, that the disastrous wife swap of recent times could be extended into something more permanent. He zapped the thought angrily. It was too easy; it was falling into Oliver's lap. And he had other plans for Oliver's lap.

But all were aware that the present arrangement was temporary, to be endured until circumstances changed, decisions made. In the meantime, he walked the map, walked the broken green lines of footpaths, the longer green dashes of the bridleways, hoof printed and punctuated with piles of ordure. He became a familiar figure for motorists to watch out for on country lanes, especially in the twilight.

On one such evening, Michael found himself in the woods surrounding Fairybridge Court. He had been pondering over the remains of a building near the gate, hitherto hidden under masses of ivy, when he became aware of a figure down by the lake, crouching down, taking a few steps and crouching again. He trained his binoculars on what turned out to be a young woman. She was carrying a bright yellow bucket and looking warily about herself every minute or so. He watched her for a while, then curious to know what she was doing, set off at a pace in her direction. He had halved the distance between them before she spotted him and made to escape. The bucket, however, impeded her progress and he soon caught up with her. She stopped and took up a defensive posture. Michael lifted his hand in a gesture of peace.

'It's okay! You've nothing to fear. I just want to know why you're here.'

'What's it got to do with you?' the girl asked. She was dark haired and pretty, or would have been had she not had various metal objects embedded in her face and a koala tattooed onto the side of her neck. Michael explained, not entirely truthfully, that he was the architect of the project about to take place on the site.

'So, you're the bastard that's going to fill in the lake!' she said.

'I assure you I am not,' Michael protested. 'In fact, if they do fill it in, they'll have to do it with me underneath! I want to restore it to its former glory, to make it a haven for wildlife. There are some councillors, among my bosses, who would get rid of it, but so far the goodies are winning.' The girl softened visibly. She scrutinised his face for clues as to character.

'So, are you going to tell me,' he continued, 'what it is you have in your bucket? Anthrax spores, radioactive isotopes?' She hesitated, then put the bucket down in front of her and took off the cloth that covered it.

'I don't know why,' she said, 'but I have a gut feeling you're OK. If I'm wrong, they'll have my guts for garters.' He peered into the bucket. On the wet moss which covered the base, crawled several miniature dinosaurs, five to six inches long, with spotty orange bellies, the shorter ones having a serrated crest down their spines. Michael gasped.

'Newts,' the girl said, 'great crested. The planners love them. With those in the lake, there's no way they'll allow it to be filled in. They're Welsh, actually. We have a newt farm in Rhayader.'

'They're beautiful,' Michael said, 'especially the ones with crests.'

'Those are the males, it's always the males who get the fancy gear.' She looked at the sky. 'Well, I'd better get on with it. It'll be dark soon.'

'I'll give you a hand,' Michael offered, fishing a Tupperware box from his rucksack. 'Where do you want to put them?'

'Just spread them out, along the edge of the lake. They don't have to be in the water.' He took his box of newts to the end of the lake and released them one at a time in the rushes. They seemed in no hurry to return to the wild, if they knew what the wild was, just lying there, pissed as newts as it were. He washed out his box in the water and returned to the girl who had also completed her task. She made to leave.

'I'd offer you a lift home,' he said, 'but I'm on foot myself.'

'That's alright. I have a bike behind the hedge near the gate. Didn't fancy lifting it over.' They walked together through the woods in the last of the daylight. 'If you work for the Council,' she asked as they approached the gate, 'would you consider keeping me up to date with developments on the site? Nothing really confidential, of course.' He laughed.

'I don't have much access to the sort of thing you're interested in,' he said, 'but yes, I don't see why not.' She scribbled a telephone number on a bus ticket she found in her pocket and gave it to him.

'And thanks for your help, Mr—?'

'Maby, Michael,' he said. 'And what are you called?'

'Amelanchier,' she told him, 'Amelanchier Jones.'

'That's an unusual name,' Michael said.

'Oh, I wouldn't say that,' she said, clambering over the locked gate, 'there's lots of us Joneses in Pontypridd.'

He waited until she had retrieved her bike from the hedge

and ridden off down the lane, before setting off in the opposite direction. He liked this girl, he decided.

* * *

Despite the parlous state of his personal life, Michael felt more relaxed at work without the civic centre and the constant stress from his relationship with Spynk, who had retreated to his office and was busy with the design of the new Council Chamber. When that was complete, an extension to the contract would be negotiated with the successful tenderer. The job of project architect had been advertised in the architectural press as a temporary post, on a higher salary than Michael's, thereby ending the slender interest he had in the project. He had also abandoned any thought of a biography of Charles Pericles Hopwood, following his discoveries in the library of the Royal Institute of British Architects. For the present, however, he had decided not to go public on Hopwood's duplicity, out of respect for his daughter, Dora's feelings. The pan, however, was simmering on the back burner.

It had not taken long for Michael to finish off his drawings of the Gypsy Site and he took them over to the Planning Department to seek the approval of Geoff Lomax before making an application. Glostover had been charged by the Government, in common with all the local authorities in England, to provide a specific number of caravan spaces within their boundaries. Being outside the Home Counties, Glostover's quota was considerable. Lomax suggested that by reducing the width of each hard standing around the perimeter by 300 mm, it would be possible to get in two extra caravans towards their allocation. He was, nevertheless, appreciative of Michael's *cottage ornée* toilet block and his landscape design. It was the first time they had met since the chapel fiasco and Lomax expressed his disquiet at the way Michael had since been treated. He had some news for him.

'This morning,' he said, 'we received an outline application from Marcus Groat, or should I say, from his wife, Virginia, for a development of eighty, three and four bedroomed houses at Fairybridge Court. Look at this!' He unfolded a site plan on the table between them. The eighty houses were laid out in informal groups of about sixteen around closes or cul-de-sacs, spreading out from a spine road, in the manner now popular with planning authorities. The houses on the extremities of the closes, at forty-five degrees to their neighbours, had desirable fan-shaped back gardens pressing against the surrounding woodland. There was a noticeably wide gap between the two houses at the far end of the spine road where it approached the open fields beyond.

It was the near end of the spine road, however, that Lomax wanted to point out. It was merely an extension to the road serving the civic centre. It ran between the main building and the chapel, severing what would have been the roofed pedestrian link between them. The access to the proposed housing development was only feasible because the chapel had gone, the Council Chamber relocated to the other side of the road.

'So,' said Michael, 'do we still accept that the chapel was demolished by accident? Or do we do something about it?' Lomax nodded slowly. Then he picked up the phone and dialled an internal number.

'Morning, Mr Jenkins, Geoff Lomax here. I wonder if you could spare a few moments to discuss a sensitive issue with Michael Maby and myself. Friday? It would be better earlier. Well, it's about Fairybridge Court. This afternoon, four thirty?' He raised his eyebrows questioningly. 'Yes, that's fine, Mr Jenkins, see you then.' He gave a thumbs up. 'No point involving my boss and Spynk, Michael, straight to the top, eh?'

* * *

Michael had never been in the chief executive's office before. It occupied a spacious room on the first floor of a Victorian villa, with Gothic windows overlooking the town park. It could have housed the entire typing pool rather than the single, albeit large and ostentatiously carved, desk, behind which Hywel Jenkins sat, his back to the windows. He was almost in silhouette, so that it was impossible to read his facial expressions. This put his visitors, the latest of these being Michael and Geoff Lomax, at a disadvantage. Their chairs were hard and uncomfortable, chosen to discourage lengthy occupation. Michael shifted his weight from one buttock to another.

'Well, gentlemen, I don't have much time but how can I help you?' Jenkins asked, pleasantly enough.

With a glance at his colleague, Lomax took up the narrative. He was brief and accurate, sticking to the facts and avoiding opinions. He had years of experience in presenting applications to planning committees. He left it to his audience to make the connections, and Hywel Jenkins made them for him.

'So, you are suggesting some sort of conspiracy theory, are you not?' he said. Lomax shrugged.

'I'm just giving you the facts, Mr Jenkins.' The chief executive turned to whom he perceived as the weaker half of the duo.

'And do you have anything to add to the argument, Mr Maby?

'Not really, I think Geoff's said it all. Except that we probably wouldn't be in this situation had more effort been made to protect the chapel when we had the chance.' Lomax put a restraining hand on Michael's knee under cover of the desk as the chief executive stiffened. This was a direct assault on himself and his lack of action. Obsequious in the company of politicians, reasonable with peers, Hywel Jenkins was a bully when it came to those he regarded as lesser mortals.

'I have been informed, Mr Maby, that you are an aficionado of this Hopwood character who, you choose to believe, was the architect of the ruinous building on the site at Fairybridge Court. I put it to you that this has coloured your judgement, to the extent that you placed the Council Chamber in an illogical relationship to the main building, a mistake that your manager, Mr Spynk, is now having to rectify. The accident which befell the chapel as you call it, was just that, an accident.'

'Furthermore, if the road serving the new building opens up an area of land for housing, then we need to look at these proposals without prejudice. Glostover is short of land suitable for housing, and we are under pressure from the government to make some available. You are attempting to weave a series of coincidences into a scandal, and I won't have it, young man, I won't have it!' He collected the papers on his desk and tapped them together, as the newscasters on television did to signify the end of a bulletin.

'So that's a no, is it, Mr Jenkins?' Michael said, rising. 'At least I know where I stand. And just for the record, I am no longer an aficionado, as you put it, of Charles Pericles Hopwood. I discovered he was a charlatan. There are lots of them about!' The chief executive appeared to be coming to the boil. Lomax hurried Michael out of the room.

'Now you've done it!' he said. 'Struck a nerve, I'd say!' Michael retrieved his drawings from Lomax's office and returned to his own, pausing only to grab his coat and a copy of the Building Design weekly before leaving. Ronnie Barge looked pointedly at his watch as he departed. On arriving home, Michael made two phone calls. The first was to Tracy at the *Glostwich Bugle*, the second to Amelanchier Jones, who wasn't in. He left her a message, then settled down with a strong coffee, to read the back pages of Building Design, Situations Vacant.

* * *

Later that same evening, by the side of a hotel pool in Marbella, former digger driver, Patrick Duffy and his wife, Maureen, sat watching the sun going down behind the palm trees. From time to time they took sips from their inappropriately named Tequila Sunrise cocktails, moving aside the little paper umbrellas to avoid nasal injury. Dinner, included in the package, awaited them. This was the life, as Pat said, more than once, to Maureen. They were both very grateful to Diggers and Shifters for retiring him early on health grounds, following what was referred to as his blackout. And their golden handshake had been extremely generous. They were thinking of investing in a small apartment just up the coast. You could live quite cheaply out here, Maureen believed. She twirled her paper umbrella between finger and thumb. Yes, this was definitely the life!

Chapter Fourteen

The telephone rang in the hallway as Virginia was passing. She picked it up, cleared her throat and announced 'Groat Hall, Virginia Groat speaking.'

'Oh, good morning, Mrs Groat,' a female voice responded. 'This is Tracy Sparks, from the *Glostwich Bugle*. I wonder if I could ask you a few questions?'

'About what?' Virginia asked cautiously.

'About your application to build eighty houses next to the new civic centre at Fairybridge Court. I understand that they will all be three and four bedroomed units. Is that correct?' Virginia knew her husband was plotting something else at Fairybridge, but the extent of the proposal caught her on the back foot. She was aware that this was dangerous ground.

'Well, the numbers are flexible at this early stage,' she said, 'and the size of the dwellings too.' Keep it vague, she told herself. Tracy probed further.

'So, some of them could be affordable, or for rent, to provide for local need? There is a shortage of small units within Glostover, particularly in Glostwich itself, I'm told.'

'I'm sure you're right, Miss Sparks, but—' Virginia was floundering. She had said enough already and could imagine Marcus's reaction when he returned. 'But I would rather you spoke to my husband about the details, and I have a cake in the

oven at the moment. He'll be in this evening. Goodbye!' She put
the phone down heavily. It was just not acceptable how Marcus
treated her, kept her in the dark. It was her land and her history.
She flounced into the drawing room. Eighty houses on the
Fairybridge estate; her uncle, Sir Penn Fairybridge, would turn
in his grave. Of course, the fortunes of the family were in decline
in his day. She knew about the Americans requisitioning of the
court, how Sir Penn had considered it his patriotic duty to comply.
She was aware of the court's destruction and the compensation
paid to her uncle, enabling him to live out his days in Mayfair.
At the end of the war the Americans had returned the land to
the family, but the connection had all but gone. The fields had
been let to a local farmer, the woods to a shooting syndicate
from Birmingham, the income helping to maintain her own
family after Sir Penn's death. There was something, however,
hovering in the back of her mind, something she had heard as a
child, discussed by her parents. She picked up the phone again
and rang her London solicitor.

* * *

Tenders for the civic centre came in during the last two days
before the deadline. They were brought in personally by each of
the contractors, the post not being trusted to ensure delivery on
time and kept unopened in the secretary's safe until the deadline
was reached. At this juncture, a small group consisting of the
Council's secretary, an elected member and Maxwell Spynk, met
in the latter's office and ceremoniously opened the tenders one
at a time, the figures recorded for posterity.

One tenderer had withdrawn with apologies. The other five's

tenders were received with shrugs and gasps, particularly by the elected member, who was not accustomed to figures with so many digits in them. As usual they were all over budget. There was a general feeling that the tenderers were being cautious, because of the uncertainty over what would happen when the Council Chamber design was finalised. The lowest tender was received from the local firm of Vogue and Randall, known in architectural circles as Vandal and Rogue. Spynk was charged with negotiating a lesser figure with their estimator and the Council's quantity surveyor, Herbert Price.

Left alone in his office, as the meeting broke up, Spynk was feeling the pressure. The re-design of the Council Chamber was not going as well as he had hoped. That afternoon he had to interview several applicants for the post of project architect, and now this. He almost wished young Maby back in his former role. He had only been obeying instructions in side-lining the fellow.

Young Maby was, at that moment, sitting at his drawing board, scratching out the demarcation lines between the caravan spaces on his site plan, and whistling, a Phil Collins number. Ronnie Barge, who was, of course, aware of Michael's demotion, and had somehow learned of his marital problems, was bemused by his apparent cheerfulness.

'You on a promise, or what?' Michael smiled and said nothing. He was thinking over the events of the previous evening when he had met up with Amelanchier and her friends in the woods at Fairybridge. They were all on foot, so that there were no cars parked in the area to attract attention. One of their number was left in the trees by the gate with a whistle, just in case of intruders. The rest of them walked down the track, between the lake and the void where the court had been There were lots of beards and long hair, some hoods, the occasional whiff of marijuana. They all had walking boots, and rucksacks on their backs, however, and could well have been taken for a party of ramblers. By the ruins of the chapel, they stopped and gathered round their leader, whom Amelanchier had introduced to Michael as Laurence. He was tall and wiry, with sharp features and a driven look about him.

'Right,' he said to the younger ones, 'you four have the bags of wildflower seed in your rucksacks. I want you to walk across the field ten paces apart, scattering the seed to both sides of you, until you reach that oak tree over there. Then turn to your right, each of you walking forty paces, and return in this direction repeating the exercise. If you hear a whistle, seal your seed bags with the bulldog clip you have in your pocket, put them in your rucksacks and return to this point. Okay, off you go!'

Michael was impressed. He was willing to bet Laurence was ex-army.

'That,' said Laurence, turning to the others, 'creates an impression of biodiversity. All common wildflowers. In your rucksacks, however, are the plugs of some genuinely threatened species, which were expensive in terms of both money and labour to produce. Handle them with care. Plant them in groups of single species as they would naturally grow, and around the edges of the field. Do not dig holes to put them in the ground. That would bring earth to the surface which could raise suspicions. Make a slot with your spade, then another slot across it, like a capital T. With your spade in the second slot, pull back on the handle which will open the first slot. Place your plug in that slot, remove the spade and firm the ground around the plant. Move on, preferably avoiding treading on your handiwork! The plants will have a hard enough time surviving without your boots to contend with.'

There were chuckles. Even more impressive, Michael thought. He set off on the vague footpath hugging the edge of the field, looking for a suitable place to plant his allocation. After a hundred metres or so, he found a nettle free area, outside the canopy of the surrounding wood. This is where I'd grow if I was a wildflower, he thought, slipping off his rucksack.

'Good choice,' said the man following him. They exchanged grins.

Michael carefully took out his tray of plugs and the telescopic spade which he had been given, again with concealment in mind. The tray had a wooden lollipop stick label, on which had been written the word 'Fritillary.' He had heard the name before, but in connection with butterflies, not flowers. He planted his plugs as instructed in an informal group. The T-slot technique worked a treat. He concertinaed his spade and stowed it in the rucksack, then strolled around the edge of the field to where Amelanchier was still working on her knees. Her tee-shirt had ridden up to reveal another tattoo on the small of her back, this one depicting a baby orangutan. She looked round at him and smiled.

'You look like you're enjoying being an activist,' she said. He was.

'Can't wait to see the flowers in bloom. What is it you're planting?'

'Some sort of orchid it says here.' She squinted at her lollipop stick. 'But it's in Latin. I'm no botanist, I just love flowers, nature in general.' He helped her to her feet, and she put a soiled hand on his shoulder to regain her balance. 'You know what, there's nothing quite like lying on your back in a wildflower meadow, with the buzzing of insects, the scent of the flowers, and nothing but the blue sky above you. You should try it.' She smelled of earth and crushed leaves. He would, he thought, love to try it. They walked back together to the others as the evening closed in.

* * *

'Definitely on a promise,' said Ronnie Barge. Michael continued scratching. In his head a figure resembling Amelanchier was skipping over a wildflower meadow towards him, like the girl in the Timotei advert. He lost the tune he was whistling and had to start again.

* * *

The shortlist for the post of project architect had been severely curtailed by the requirement that the applicants were able to start work almost immediately. Persons in a job already would have had to give their present employer two months' notice, and Vogue and Randall were champing at the bit to start work on site. It was also a temporary post which would have deterred many potential applicants, despite the generous salary being offered. Spynk had found only four persons worth interviewing. He and the Personnel Officer, now to be referred to as the Human Resources Manager, despite the implication that humans were disposable raw materials like roadstone and sand, sat glumly in Spynk's office, awaiting the next applicant.

They had already interviewed a sixty-seven-year-old retiree whose wife was fed up with him hanging around the house and questioning her established routines. He was well behind the times with current legislation and had a hearing problem. He wondered why a Slavic Centre was required in Glostwich, were there many eastern European immigrants in the town? 'Nice to meet you, Mr Stink,' he said on leaving.

The second applicant, a Mr M'Boto, who had been shortlisted mainly for reasons of political correctness, proved to be very competent and personable. He stated from the off, however, that he was a Precambrian Lollard and needed to have Fridays off for door-to-door evangelism. He was prepared for a proportionate reduction of the stated salary, but as Spynk pointed out, the Contractor would very quickly identify that Friday was the day for nefarious practices. He was therefore eliminated.

The third applicant did not turn up, which left a Ms Julia Faraday, whose CV explained that she was returning to full-time work after an extensive break, her child now being eligible for nursery care. Spynk was not hopeful, having doubts about the ability of a woman to stand up to an unscrupulous contractor and his hairy-arsed workforce. He quickly revised his opinion, however, when it became evident that Ms Faraday was interviewing him, rather than the reverse. She transfixed him with her gaze, holding him back from his usual technique of angel spotting, focussing on every word he uttered. That she would cause a stir on an exclusively male building site was indisputable, the word voluptuous coming to mind. She had obviously kept up to date with developments in architecture and the building industry during her absence. Spynk could not find a reason for not employing her. He decided against asking her about further children, the contract being little longer than the average pregnancy, and he sensed that she would bridle at the question in any case. After a brief discussion in her absence with the Human Resources Manager, he called her back in and offered her the job. She accepted with an easy grace that implied there had never been any doubt in her mind that she would get it.

* * *

'Damn woman,' Marcus Groat growled, returning to the drawing room after answering a call from the *Bugle*, 'seems to think we'll be including some social housing in the development at Fairybridge.' Virginia was relieved that his misogyny was this time directed at Tracy Sparks.

'Would that not be the right thing for Glostwich? Young people need somewhere to live, and they can't afford anything around here. They have to leave their families and move to London or Birmingham.'

'Bloody good thing too,' said Groat, 'get on their bikes! Who wants a council house next to them? Broken down cars and neglected front gardens! Knocks thousands off the value of your house!' He stormed off to his study. Virginia knew there was no point in arguing with him – there were other ways of skinning a cat. She smiled to herself. Tomorrow, she was off to London all by herself, on a shopping trip to all intents and purposes. But Mrs Virginia Groat, niece of the late Sir Penn Fairybridge, had an appointment in Grosvenor Square.

Chapter Fifteen

Spynk and Herbert Price had several meetings with Vogue and Randall to discuss measures to reduce the tender figure down to an acceptable level. Changes to the plan or the structure were quickly ruled out because of a knock-on effect, involving much work and further delays. The axe fell mainly on internal finishes, cheap vinyl tiles replacing carpet and hardwood floors, the textured wall finishes in the foyer downgraded to emulsion paint. Smart back to the wall sanitary ware with concealed cisterns disappeared from staff toilets. What was wrong with utilitarian close-coupled loos and exposed plumbing? The landscaping, including Michael's Cappadocian Maple, was completely omitted. There were plenty of existing trees around, were there not, and grass required less maintenance than plant beds.

Eventually, a revised price was agreed, and the contract signed by both parties, with handshakes and a general bonhomie, as was usual before the commencement of building works on site. Vogue and Randall then took over the Fairybridge site and erected a secure compound in which to store their plant and materials, their site office and portaloo. For the first few days the clerk of works, Arthur Brickbat, stood in for the Council and kept an eye on their progress. Despite the good weather he made a point of being in the office when the new project architect arrived to take up her responsibilities.

Spynk brought her around and introduced her to the staff.
'Julia Faraday, this is Michael Maby – Ronnie Barge – Arthur
Brickbat.' She shook hands firmly with them all. Then Spynk
took her into the next office to meet the others. Arthur's eyes
were popping.

'Did you see the jugs on that?' he gasped. Ronnie snorted.

'She won't last the week on site.' He quickly changed his mind
on that score. Julia returned alone and hung her coat and handbag
behind the door. Then she walked over to Ronnie's desk, removed
the calendar from the wall facing him and dropped it in the bin.

'We won't be needing that.' Ronnie was speechless. The
calendar bore the name of Orifice Plumbing Products and had
been given to him by their representative the previous Christmas.
It pictured a young lady in an Orifice shower cubicle, face turned
ecstatically up into the spray, and was, he considered, in the best
of taste owing to the discrete positioning of a large lathery sponge
in her left hand.

'You can't do that!' he said.

'I just did,' she said. 'Now, Michael, I know the civic centre
was your baby. I would be grateful if you could spare an hour to
go through it with me. And Arthur, I think you would be better
employed out on site. I'll see you there later.'

Brickbat left meekly. He considered it his duty to warn
the contractor what was in store for him. What was the world
coming to?

Julia pulled up a stool to Michael's board, and they poured
over the civic centre drawings one at a time in detail, referring
occasionally to the Bills of Quantity, Ronnie maintaining an
offended silence in the background. When they came to the end
of the pile, Julia sat back and studied Michael's face.

'Well,' she said, 'I have to say, I don't like it.' Ronnie grunted. Michael, however, nodded.

'It's a camel,' he said, 'it started life as a horse, and became a camel.'

'My thoughts entirely.' Julia moved the last of the sheets onto his laying out space and noticed the gypsy site drawing on the board beneath. 'Now this is nice,' she said, pointing at the community building which housed the washing and toilet facilities. 'Very *cottage ornée*. In fact, a little gem! Some people, I suppose, would say it was wasted on travellers?'

'Oh, they do,' he said, glancing at Ronnie, 'they certainly do!'

Michael had lost interest in the civic centre, and in number twenty-four, Goose Green too. The domestic arrangements which had been in place since his discovery of Andrea's infidelity, were proving unsustainable. Little things like both wanting to use the washing machine at the same time, or neither of them putting out the bins in time, grew to ridiculous proportions. Housework was neglected, the garden was knee deep in weeds.

One evening Andrea stormed into the lounge where Michael was watching the early evening news with a takeaway *tikka masala* on his lap, and announced she wanted a divorce.

'Fine,' he said, forking a spicy morsel of chicken into his mouth and proceeding to chew it before continuing. 'But on my terms. After all, you're the adulterer, not me!' Andrea hissed through her teeth.

'And what about the Ladies Evening?'

'What about it indeed! Nothing happened to me. How about you?'

She stormed out again. Moments later the front door slammed behind her.

He finished his takeaway, then rang Jane and told her the news. It seemed she had not taken any action yet but was seriously considering it. They agreed that it could be beneficial to synchronise their petitions, though using two different solicitors to avoid accusations of collusion.

'And I want you to know,' Michael told her, 'that I would very much like to take you out for a drink somewhere, but if we were seen together, it could be used against us.' There was silence. Then Jane said quietly,

'You're probably right, Michael.' She didn't sound convinced.

Michael put the phone down and bent to pick up an official looking letter behind the front door, that he must have missed when he came home. It was from the National Record Office, a response to an enquiry he had made and paid for several weeks previously, a certified copy of an entry of death. It read:

When and where died: 10 May 1900, Mafeking, Cape Provinces, S. Africa.

Name and surname: James Edward Cranham.

Sex: male.

Age: 25 years.

Occupation: architect/voluntary soldier.

Cause of death: bullet wound to chest.

Signature, description and residence of informant: Captain Hugh Dodgson.

Now of Chigley Manor, Hampshire.

When registered: 20 June 1900

Signature of registrar: Philip Smyth

There was a note enclosed:

Captain Dodgson recorded the death of James Cranham at his local registrar's office on returning to England. He left a brief description of the circumstances: James Cranham was killed in an attempt to break through the Boer lines to link up with the relieving English forces. He showed great courage and will be sadly missed by his comrades.

* * *

At Fairybridge, Vogue and Randall were making an excellent start, mainly because the basement had already been dug out for them. The good weather was holding out, but they had pumps on site to deal with any flooding. They cut out shallow trenches around the perimeter and on the lines of internal loadbearing walls and laid out steel reinforcement in accordance with the structural engineer's drawings. Then for the next three days a fleet of ready-mix lorries brought in loads of viscous concrete which was pumped into the hole and raked around by a gang of ground workers. At the end of the first two weeks of the contract a uniform concrete raft covered the whole of the excavation's floor.

The builders had taken heed of Arthur Brickbat's warning, and whenever Julia Faraday appeared on site she was treated with deference by Jim Randall and his site agent, Mick Mulvey. No-one, however, thought to tell the bricklayers, who then arrived on site and began to build a concrete block wall around the perimeter. The weather was still fine and from time to time one or other of the brickies burst loudly into song, then stopped abruptly, in the manner of his trade. They were happy in their work. When an attractive pair of legs appeared above eye level on the edge of the excavation, a chorus of wolf-whistles ensued.

The following day, a different gang of brickies started where the first gang had left off. This time they were briefed by Jim Randall himself.

* * *

There was a recorded message on Michael's phone when he came home from work, from Amelanchier at her parents' house. He rang back. A gruff Welsh voice answered. No, she wasn't in, was that Ivan speaking? No? He left a message for her to ring him again. Eventually, later in the evening, Amelanchier contacted him.

'Just wondered,' she said, 'whether you would like to join us for a demo in Herefordshire this weekend? There's a company down there who do horrible experiments on live animals.' He was cautious, but curious.

'Who's us, and how many of you are there? She laughed.

'You never know who'll turn up. They're just people who see things in a similar way, like me and, I hope, like you. And besides, you have a car. It's a long way to Ledbury.'

'So, it's not my commitment you're after.'

'No, just your body! To swell the ranks, of course.' He agreed to pick her up early on Saturday morning. She gave him an address.

'And who's Ivan?'

'Oh, he's just one of the mob. You met him at Fairybridge. He'll be coming with us in the car.' She rang off before he could change his mind.

* * *

The evening after the second gang of brickies had started on the site, Mick Mulvey reported into Vogue and Randall's office. Jim Randall quizzed him. Had Boadicea been on site and did the men behave themselves this time?

The answer to both questions was yes.

'Thank God for that,' said Randall.

'To be honest,' his site agent opined, 'I thought she looked a bit disappointed. We had some other visitors too.'

'What sort of visitors?' Randall looked concerned.

'Well, one of them was from the Department of the Environment. He showed me his card, looked through the drawings and wandered around the excavations. He brought his own safety helmet. Didn't say much, just thanked me and left.'

'And the others?'

'Two of them. Looked like professors, tweed jackets and brown brogue shoes. One of them had a white beard. They didn't come on the site itself. Spent a lot of time peering into the lake, then moved into the field beyond it, the one with the big oak tree in the middle.'

'Don't sound like anything to worry us,' said Randall, 'it's the Health and Safety buggers we've got to watch out for. Okay, Mick, see you tomorrow.' He turned to the invoice from the Builders Merchant that he was reading. 'How much? For concrete blocks? They've got to be joking!'

* * *

On Saturday morning Michael drove down to Ledbury with Amelanchier in the passenger seat perusing his road atlas. It was not very far, and he knew the town had a railway station, so maybe it wasn't just his car she was interested in. Ivan sat in the back. Michael remembered him from the wildflower planting at Fairybridge. He was a slender, intense looking young man who didn't say much, but nevertheless managed to convey his contempt for cars and the bourgeoisie who drove them, especially those who Amelanchier seemed to favour.

Arriving in the town they parked in a supermarket carpark where dozens of beat-up cars and vans were already disgorging their fellow protestors and their placards. *Murderers,* the placards read, and *Animals Also Feel Pain.* The protestors were mainly young, but with a sprinkling of the middle-aged and even pensioners. They wore a medley of clothing, loose and casual, yet instantly identifiable as the uniform of dissension. Michael felt a little overdressed. He recognised Laurence among the growing crowd, forming it into a column, four persons wide. When sufficient folk had arrived, the column moved off, he, Amelanchier, Ivan and the man who had approved his choice of planting site at Fairybridge, alongside each other.

They tramped into the town centre, by the clock tower and the market hall on stilts, chanting the name of the hated laboratory, 'Colitox, Colitox,' and turned north up the main street. Cars pulled into the kerb at crazy angles, shoppers took refuge in Woolworths and the NatWest bank. Some, whose family members had found much needed employment with the laboratory and its suppliers, hurled abuse at them from the pavement. They hurled abuse back. At the end of town reinforcements poured off the railway station and tagged on to the end of the column. *Colitox, Colitox.* By this time the front ranks had reached the laboratory gates which closed as they neared. Uniformed men watched from behind the protecting three-metre-high security fence, topped with strands of razor wire angled towards the road.

A dense and noisy throng of protestors formed in front of the laboratory gates and extending fifty metres in either direction. Then they sat down in the road, holding their placards aloft. *Sadists, Gays Against Vivisection, Torture Your Own Kids,* they said. Cars carrying would-be shoppers approached, carried out five-point turns, and made for Bromyard instead. Lorries came from the motorway through the town and crept right up the outer protestors, aiming to intimidate them. Nobody budged. The lorry drivers wound down their windows and lambasted the crowd from the safety of their cabs. Someone started singing to drown the abuse. 'We Shall Overcome,' 'Kumbaya,' and somewhat incongruously, 'You'll Never Walk Alone.'

Then over the singing a siren could be heard, followed by a second and a third. Blue flashing lights reflected off windows and road signs as the police arrived. A terse request from a megaphone, for the crowd to disperse, was ignored. Someone threw a sod at one of the police cars. All hell broke out. Policemen waded into the throng, picking out the obvious leaders and the ones who refused to stand up and move, among them Laurence and Ivan, and bundling them into a large van that had arrived.

'Pigs,' Amelanchier shouted at a red-faced constable, who turned and made towards her. Michael grabbed her hand and dragged her away, still bad-mouthing the police, towards the town, the shouting fading behind them. Delving off the road, they found themselves on a sunken tree lined path, gently curving in the general direction, Michael surmised, of the carpark, and slowed to walking pace. There were few other people around. Amelanchier was elated.

'What about Ivan?' he asked her.

'Oh, don't worry about him,' she said. 'He's a big boy now.

He'll find his own way home. It's not the first time he's been nabbed by the Fuzz.'

His sense of direction proved correct. Reaching the carpark, they looked right and left, then strolled nonchalantly back to his car. Michael consulted the road atlas.

'We'll go home via Malvern,' he decided. 'That way we'll avoid the police. And it's a nice run along the hills.'

'I'm always up for the scenic route,' Amelanchier said. They drove out into the countryside and were soon travelling up the long rise towards the stepped terraces of the Herefordshire Beacon, or British Camp as it was known. At the point where the road crossed the ridge of the hills, where walkers sat with their pints outside a large pub, they turned left.

'I know this place,' said Amelanchier suddenly,' I've been here before, another demo, couple of years ago. Big house, a bit further down the road. They used to breed beagles for experiments with cigarette smoking, like the tobacco industry didn't know already their products killed you! Look, this is the place.' They pulled into a drive entrance. There was a padlocked gate with the house name on it – Perrycroft. 'They had to close down eventually,' Amelanchier said, 'after sixty of their beagles suffocated in a lorry heading for the continent. There was a national outcry.'

'I remember,' Michael said. There was something else about this place gnawing at his memory. Then it came to him. Perrycroft, the Voysey house that had inspired James Cranham to enter the competition. He told Amelanchier the story, about James abandoning the scheme and leaving the country after his fiancée had jilted him, how Hopwood had stolen the design to springboard his career, how, and here despite himself, his voice cracked, James had died at the Siege of Mafeking. She listened quietly, then put an arm around his shoulders and gently kissed his cheek.

'It's alright, Michael, it's alright! Let's go and look at the place.'

They climbed over the gate and walked down through the trees to the house. It was authentic Voysey, long horizontal windows, subdivided into vertical lights, tall tapering chimneys, white rendered walls. But the paintwork was peeling, the render falling off, Maud Jekyll's gardens lost in brambles and weeds. And dominating the whole, the black sheds where the beagles had howled for their freedom. Perrycroft needed a new and caring owner.

The afternoon sun had come around to the west when they returned to the car, and they became aware that the whole hillside on the other side of the road was an intense blue. They just hadn't been looking in that direction before. Fingers of blue stretched off into groves of newly leaved birch and hazel. A heavy perfume filled the air. It was impossible to be depressed.

'Come on then, Michael Maby.' She waited impatiently in the road while he made sure the car was locked. Then they set off on a rising path through the bluebells, hand in hand where the width of the path allowed. The view from the top was spectacular, rolling Herefordshire countryside looking west, the broad vale of the Severn, Bredon Hill and the Cotswold escarpment to the east. Being weekend there were many walkers along the ridge but departing from the path on the way back they found a secluded hollow on the edge of the trees. The koala and the orangutan, it soon emerged, were not the only tattoos on Amelanchier's body. He touched them in wonderment. They were strangely erotic. He wasn't so sure, however, about the ironmongery.

Chapter Sixteen

Retribution soon followed. On Monday morning Michael was summoned to the chief executive's office. Jenkins slapped a copy of the Marches Journal on the desk in front of him.

'Is this how you think a responsible officer of Glostover District Council should behave?'

Michael pulled the paper towards him. A photograph on the front page clearly showed Amelanchier and himself running from the mêlée outside the Colitox laboratory. It had been taken from the railway bridge with a telephoto lens. His face was upturned towards the camera. Amelanchier was laughing. There was no point in denying it.

'What I do in my own time at weekends, Mr Jenkins, is no concern of the Council, or of yours for that matter. I broke no laws and I firmly believe that the activities of Colitox are morally wrong.' The chief executive flushed.

'Morals, Mr Maby, have nothing to do with it. We are talking about the neutrality of officers, who are charged with carrying out the political decisions of our elected members, not those of ourselves. I have had enough of your attitude. You will return to your office where Mr Spynk will ensure that you clear your desk and leave. You will receive two months' salary in due course. From this moment, Mr Maby, you are no longer an employee of this Council! Goodbye!'

So, Michael found himself driving home, on the passenger seat beside him his briefcase with his drawing instruments, a few architectural magazines and a solar powered calculator, the property of Glostover District Council. In recognition of his time with the latter, he had received a shake of his hand from Ronnie Barge, a few formal words from Maxwell Spynk addressed to the ever-present angel behind him, and, surprisingly, a peck on the cheek from Julia Faraday. He was already forming in his mind the case for claiming wrongful dismissal. His part in the demonstration was patently just a convenient excuse for Jenkins to get rid of him.

That evening Andrea made one of her increasingly infrequent visits. There was a look of triumph on her face, and he knew why.

'So, you're as white as the driven snow, are you? Never showed any interest in other women? And now you're involved with a hippy. Bit of a goer, is she? Into drugs and free love? My solicitor will be really interested in that young lady!'

Michael went out for a walk until she'd collected whatever she'd come for. Oliver was sitting in his silver green Corsair around the corner. He walked past without acknowledging him, resisting an urge to kick in the rear door panel. When he returned, the car and Andrea had gone, and the phone was ringing. It was Dora Hopwood Brown. She wanted to know if he had made any progress with her father's biography.

What could he say! That he had discovered her father was a plagiarist, that he had abandoned the biography project, probably for good?

'I haven't been able to do much, I'm afraid. I've been too busy recently,' he said lamely, 'but I'll have plenty of time on my hands now.' He immediately regretted his comment.

'Oh, why's that?' she asked. He screwed up his eyes. He had to tell.

'I've been sacked,' he said, 'and Andrea's left me.'

'Michael!' The old lady was plainly taken aback. 'What happened?'

'Well, I was spotted at a demo, and my boss—'

'Never mind your job, you can get another of those. What happened with your wife?'

'She was seeing someone, supposedly a friend, and I found out.'

'I'm sorry,' Dora said after a pause,' But the signs were there, were they not?'

'I suppose so, but I didn't see them.'

'No, we see what we want to see, don't we?' Dora said quietly. 'And I interrupted you talking about your boss.' Michael hesitated before replying.

'I think there's some sort of corruption going on in the Council, something involving the chief executive and a prominent councillor. And they know I'm onto it. So, they found something to lay on me.'

'Sounds like the Pargetters,' said Dora, 'they wield a lot of power. My father was one of them, you know. Best out of it, Michael. Why don't you set up on your own?'

'You're not the first person to make that suggestion,' Michael said darkly. 'Incidentally, I did manage to discover what happened to your Aunt Isabel's fiancée. He was a hero, died in the Boer War.'

'Really?' Dora was quiet again. 'That rings a bell. I vaguely remember Aunt Isabel disappearing off to South Africa in the middle of her suffragette activity. Quite unexpectedly. It had something to do with her estrangement from the family. My father tried to dissuade her, the Boers, which I thought were some sort of wild pig, were still active. It was too dangerous, he said.' *I'll bet he did,* thought Michael.

* * *

The Fairybridge Housing outline proposal was going before Planning Committee the following Tuesday evening. Tiring of job applications and the tailoring of his CV to suit each of them, Michael decided to exercise his right as a member of the public to attend. When he arrived, the committee room was crowded with councillors and several applicants, wandering around and peering at drawings pinned to the mobile display boards placed strategically around the room, in a way that suggested they understood what they were looking at. He snuck in and found a seat at the back of the hall, just before the chairman called for order, and the crowd gradually seated itself.

It was odd, sitting among the public behind the elected members and facing his former colleagues on the dais. Michael spotted Tracy from the *Bugle*, who waved a finger at him. Geoff Lomax caught his eye and winked. The chief executive perused the floor, his glance passing over Michael then abruptly returning to his face. He frowned. It was not his custom to attend Planning Meetings, but it was his prerogative to do so. Marcus Groat arrived just before proceedings began, and took a seat near the door, which was then closed by the committee clerk.

The first item concerned an application to construct a bedroom and en-suite over an existing garage, which the planning officer had recommended for approval. The people living opposite had approached their local member who stated that the extension would spoil their view and should be rejected. The planning officer explained that neighbours had a right of light but that no one's view was sacrosanct. The committee passed the application, and the people living opposite, who were sitting in front of Michael got up and departed, grumbling.

Next came an application for a change of use from redundant joinery workshops to holiday lets in a village close to Glostwich. There were representations against the proposal from village residents, one of whom owned an existing holiday let, concerning increased traffic on the roads, unsuitable access and the end of rural life as they knew it. The landlord of the village pub, which was within walking distance, however, was very much in favour. It was decided to turn down the application for three units and advise the owner to reapply for two.

A listed building application concerning a picture window in a barn conversion was rejected, and another landlord was told he could not replace the 1960s steel windows in his eighteenth-century inn with period hardwood alternatives because the steel windows were part of the inn's history.

Michael's attention wandered. The Christmas streamer remnant was still Blu-Tacked to the beam above him. Plumbing noises interrupted the various speakers' contributions. He looked along the row of people to his right to see if there was anyone he recognised. The woman next to him tugged her skirt toward her knees. A distinguished looking gentleman further down the row, with white hair and carefully tended beard, consulted his notes. And turning to his left he noticed a closely cropped and sturdy man, probably in his fifties, wearing a high lapelled jacket, with a yellow bow tie and an air of authority. He wondered why they were there.

Eventually the meeting reached the item on the agenda concerned with the proposed Fairybridge housing development. At this point, Marcus Groat, rose to his feet, ostentatiously declared an interest, and left the building with a smug glance in the direction of the chief executive.

Geoff Lomax drew the attention of the assembly to the board on which was pinned the site plan Michael had seen in the planner's office.

'Before we go any further,' he said, 'I should emphasise that this is an outline application, and that should you approve it much more detail will be required before full planning permission is granted. What we are here to consider is the need for such a development in the district, and whether the proposed site is the right place to build it.' He paused to emphasise the point. 'The proposal is for eighty houses. As you know, the country, and Glostover in particular, has a substantial housing need, which is likely to be exacerbated by the new hypermarket you have approved on Glostwich Pastures Retail Park. These eighty houses would substantially contribute to that need. I do consider that making them all three and four bedrooms is not socially acceptable, and that you should stipulate that ten to twenty per cent should be smaller, affordable units.'

'Hear, hear!' said the one socialist councillor, with murmurs of approval from several of the independent/liberal minority.

'As for the Fairybridge site,' Lomax continued, 'it is not within Glostover's Development Plan, but it is next to the civic centre which is currently under construction, and which may well set a precedent. And the road serving that centre provides good vehicular access to the proposed residential site. It is not at present within a Conservation Area, nor a designated Area of Natural Beauty. And the density of the housing proposed conforms with our policy.' He lowered the pad from which he was reading.

'Well,' said the deputy chairman of the Council, 'as Mr Lomax has told us, this is a proposal in principle only and it appears that there is a good case for approving it. I therefore move that—' Lomax interrupted him.

'With respect, Councillor, there is another side to the debate. I have had requests to address the meeting from two experts in different fields who are, I see, in the room tonight. Is it the committee's wish that they should be allowed to do so?' Faces turned towards the seats behind them. The deputy chairman was miffed.

'Well, if you think that's really necessary?' Lomax nodded firmly. He shrugged. 'Then carry on!' Lomax gestured to the white-haired gentleman in the back row.

'This is Professor Carrington, who is the head of botany at the University of Mid-Wales.' The professor stood and raised his notes in acknowledgement.

'Thank you, Mr Lomax,' he said. 'I was asked, ladies and gentlemen, to investigate the flora of the meadow, being the site of this proposed development, which I did. And I have to say, even as a botanist with many years' experience, that its biodiversity is impressive. On a short visit I was able to identify twenty-four different species of wildflower. Now, I don't wish to overwhelm you with a list of Latin names, so I will just mention some of the common versions with which you will probably be more familiar. There are fritillaries, several species of orchids and the very rare Maiden's Frogwort, apart from the more widespread bluebells, cowslips, campions, etc, etc. Meadows of this quality are fast disappearing from the English countryside, and I consider that ploughing up of this habitat and its replacement with housing would be an act of desecration. The construction of the adjoining civic centre is already threatening the natural environment. My colleague, a zoologist at the university, has found great crested newts in the nearby lake, and more than one grass snake.' The woman next to Michael shuddered.

'I believe,' concluded the professor, 'that far from building on this field, you should be designating it as a Site of Special Scientific Interest! I will be leaving a copy of my report for the records.' There was a stunned silence.

'Could you tell us, Professor,' the chief executive asked, 'who it was that requested you to investigate the site?'

'I could, but I won't,' said Professor Carrington, 'that is confidential information.' He sat down again. Jenkins fixed Michael with a baleful stare.

'Thank you, Professor,' said Geoff Lomax. 'Now we also have with us, Mr Johannsen, from the American Embassy in London. To save members straining their necks any further, Mr Johannsen, would you like to come to the front to address them?'

The man with the yellow bow tie made his way forward, amidst a flurry of speculation from the assembly. An American, in Glostwich? Michael noted the cut of his jacket, with a seam down the back. On the dais he turned to face the members. Unlike the professor he had no notes.

'Good evening, gentlefolk,' he said in a deep rich voice. The woman next to Michael shuddered again. 'Some of you, or maybe your parents, will remember that there were many of my countrymen based around here during the Second World War. Your fine stately home, Fairybridge Court, was taken over by the US Army for the duration and was used for the storage of arms and ammunition. But an unfortunate accident occurred and a fire destroyed the court. As a result,' Johannsen paused, 'six GIs lost their lives.'

Officers gasped; a sympathetic murmur ran through the room. That part of the story was not generally known. Michael had certainly not heard it before.

'Now, you have to remember,' said Johannsen, 'that this was 1944, on the eve of D-Day. There were other fish to fry. So, the casualties were buried where they fell, here in the grounds of Fairybridge Court, in the meadow where you are considering allowing a housing development to be built.' He paused again to let the news sink in.

'You may think that we could just disinter those bodies and take them back to the United States. Well, we have managed to contact the families, mainly distant, great nieces and nephews, one grandson, and they all feel that it is wrong to disturb those guys again, and that they should stay where they are with their comrades. And I should point out that the compensation paid to Lord Fairybridge at the end of the war took into account the land still occupied, as it were, by my countrymen. This is sacred ground, folks!'

Through the window Michael could see Marcus Groat pacing up and down in the carpark. He would have expected to be called back in by now. Fred Hatton, the socialist councillor, rose to his feet, uncharacteristically serious.

'Well, that sheds a different light on things, does it not? Supporting this proposal makes us not only spoilers of the environment but desecrators of burial grounds too. And I for one will vote against it.' He sat down, as Councillor Robert Snow rose to speak.

'For once I completely agree with Councillor Hatton. This proposal is just not acceptable.' Other members began to fall in line. If Robert Snow, arch capitalist and entrepreneur was against the development, then it must be wrong. And Robert Snow recognised an opportunity to ride the tide of public opinion when he saw it. He glanced at the reporter from the *Bugle*, Tracy Somebody, scribbling furiously in her pad. 'How could we claim to have a special relationship with America if we desecrate the graves of the brave soldiers they sent to defend us in the Second World War?'

A vote was taken and the proposal to build eighty homes at Fairybridge was refused by fifteen votes to nil with three abstentions. Then Marcus Groat was called back in.

Chapter Seventeen

Hywel Jenkins sat in his office, staring gloomily out of his window at the ordinary people going about their business in the park, young mums with their pushchairs, joggers jogging, pensioners sitting on benches decrying the lack of public toilets in the town. He dreamed of his boyhood, of building dens on the mountain, as the modest hill behind his hometown in South Wales was known. No interference, just dead branches, turves and bracken. If only civic centres and housing estates were that easy, and he and his pals could just get on with the job. A chief executive's lot was not a happy one. Was it his fault that the Planning Committee had thrown out Groat's housing estate? Did he deserve the chairman's tirade in the carpark after the meeting? No, he had no idea how the American Embassy had got involved, though he had his suspicions about the intervention of the professor of botany. He sipped his coffee and took a bite of his digestive biscuit, just as the phone rang.

'Mr O'Rourke to see you, sir,' his PA announced.

'Okay, send him in.' A crumb had lodged in his throat, and he was still coughing when the Council's treasurer entered. He gestured towards a chair and took another sip of coffee. It was only when his throat cleared that he noticed the treasurer's face, which was ashen.

'Good God, George, whatever is the matter? You look like you've seen the Grim Reaper!'

'Worse than that, Hywel, an inspector from the Ministry. Their auditors have been looking into our books.' He swallowed. 'It seems that the windfall we identified last year, with which we are financing the new civic centre at Fairybridge, has to be considered when determining our allocation for the next financial year. In other words, our allocation will be reduced by the full value of the windfall. We have a problem, Hywel, a big problem!'

A knot began to tighten in Jenkins' intestines. Or so it felt. More bad news and this one was a humdinger. He picked up the phone.

'Ring round the chief officers, Marilyn. I want them all in my office at two o'clock this afternoon. No excuses. No prior commitments. This is an emergency!'

* * *

At Fairybridge, site agent Mick Mulvey was amazed to see from his office window, a black limousine and several other cars pull into his temporary carpark. A number of suited men and women in smart dresses and heeled shoes emerged and walked cautiously over the rough gravel, past his site and towards the meadow beyond. Some were carrying wreaths and bouquets of flowers. Julia Faraday detached herself from the party and hurried over to the site office.

'It's an impromptu memorial service,' she explained, 'didn't have time to warn you. Evidently, there are six Americans buried here from the Second World War.' She dashed off to catch up with the others, who not being sure of the location of the graves, were congregating under the oak tree. She joined Michael on the edge of the group, which included the man from the American embassy, Johannsen, Virginia Groat, several councillors and the Reverend Rickets from the local church. Tracy Sparks was there, representing the Press. It was a short and simple service, Johannsen repeated the story, then read out the names of the GIs, and the States from which they came. The reverend blessed them, then floral tributes were placed around the bole of the tree. An awkward silence ensued, then people began returning to their cars.

Michael approached Johannsen and took out from the bag he was carrying, one of the brass and cast-iron rosettes which had been found in the ruins of the court. He explained.

'These were part of the staircase balustrade in the court. There are six of them here and I thought it would be appropriate if you gave one to each of the soldiers' families as a keepsake.' The tough American was visibly moved.

'Well, thank you, sir! That will be much appreciated. I will personally make sure that the families ged 'em!' He handed the bag to his driver. 'And who do I tell them donated the rosettes? Michael Maby? Thank you again, Michael. I will not forget your gesture!'

Virginia Groat had overheard the exchange. She touched Michael on the shoulder as he was walking away.

'You're the young architect my husband talked about, aren't you? I think you have been badly treated! And that was a lovely thing to do, giving those rosettes to the Americans.' Michael shrugged.

'I suppose they were not mine to give,' he said, 'but there are more if you would like them.'

'I would. I would, Michael! Maybe you could drop them off sometime?'

'Good move, that, Michael,' whispered Julia, as she passed, 'did you no harm at all.' He shook his head. People were so cynical these days.

* * *

It was an unusually subdued group of chief officers that congregated in the chief executive's office that afternoon. They had heard the rumours. It fell to the treasurer to explain the problem and its implications. After all, reasoned the chief executive, it was George's misinformation that had led to the situation in the first place. He sat back and watched his treasurer squirm. There were groans and sighs as the story unfurled.

'So, savings will have to be made,' Jenkins said, when the narrative had drawn to an unhappy end, 'unless, of course, we drastically increase the Council Tax.' A shudder ran through the assembly. They remembered the Poll Tax and the riots which followed it.

'The councillors would never approve that in any case,' said the secretary. There was general agreement. 'We could close the library and public toilets,' he continued. This met with half-hearted approval. The two bookshops in the town were struggling, and a library of free books didn't help their situation. Public toilets, however, were a different matter.

'How about reducing the housing programme and putting up rents in existing public housing?' suggested the solicitor, who had a negligible budget and relished the thought of his colleagues losing some clout. The housing manager was dismissive.

'No way, José! But we could postpone the gypsy camps that the government is pushing on us. We just can't find any suitable sites, can we?' The technical services officer reminded him that the first site was already designed and ready to go out to tender. The others ignored his intervention. Why should they spend good money on travellers, putting pressure on the schools and increasing the local crime rate, when nothing came back in the form of rent or rates?

'So, what about requesting the staff to forego their next year's annual salary rises?' asked the chief planner, who was fairly new to the job and a regular church goer. There were hoots of laughter.

'Imagine what the Union would say about that,' said the secretary.

'Well, we could lead by example,' persisted the chief planner, 'take a small cut in our salaries.' The others stared at him in amazement. Hurriedly the treasurer intervened.

'I'm sorry, gentlemen, but we're just playing round the edges of the problem. There's only one thing we can do to rectify the matter.' He paused. 'And that is to terminate the contract for the civic centre!'

After a long silence, the technical services officer spoke.

'We would have to pay for the basement which is almost complete, and the clearance of the original ruins has already been paid for.'

'And there will be considerable compensation for breach of contract,' warned the solicitor, 'not to mention the purchase price of the land.'

'Could the previous owner be persuaded to buy it back?' asked the chief planner. 'As a serving councillor of this authority, does he not have some moral obligation to do so?' There were more incredulous stares.

'I think we can discount that possibility,' said the chief

executive firmly, 'Mr Groat will not be feeling very charitable at present. No, George is right, we will have to pull the plug on the civic centre, but all of us will have to consider sacrifices within our departments too. Early retirements, voluntary redundancies, the merging of some services, the privatising of others. I strongly feel, for instance, that the Architects' Section must go. We won't be doing much building in the near future, and there are plenty of local private practices to step in if we do need them.'

The technical services officer, whose department included the architects, was about to protest but thought better of it. He was sixty and early retirement had been mentioned.

'I want every one of you,' continued the chief executive, 'to come up with a fully costed proposal of savings to be made in each of your departments by tomorrow night. We will meet here at six thirty. I will call an extraordinary meeting of the Council for the following day. All work on the civic centre will be suspended immediately.' He looked directly at the treasurer. 'And some of us need to consider falling on our swords!'

* * *

Michael had left a message for Amelanchier after the planning meeting and twenty-four hours later she rang him back. Her father had evidently forgotten to pass the message on, and she had just found his scribbled note.

'That's alright,' Michael said, 'I just wanted to tell you that the housing development at Fairybridge was thrown out, thanks partly to your professor's report. Where did you find him?'

'Oh, he's Ivan's uncle, actually. But he is a professor of botany. Very useful from time to time. He got me into wildflowers.'

'And then you got me into them. Bluebells, weren't they?' She laughed.

'I didn't hear you complain.'

'Well, I feel I need to know more about biodiversity,' Michael said, 'why don't I pick you up this evening and bring you around to my house for some further tuition, and a glass or two of wine?'

'Why don't you, indeed? About seven thirty, okay?' She blew him a kiss over the phone. 'Look forward to it.' He put the phone down and headed for the walk-in cupboard where they, he, kept the vacuum cleaner. An hour to dust and hoover, another to catch up with the washing up, make the bed and stuff his discarded clothes into the washing machine. Why all the fuss about housework? He did a quick tour around the house before he left. Yes, it all looked pretty good, his domestic skills had not deserted him.

He needn't have bothered. On his return with Amelanchier, the front door had hardly closed behind them when she began to unbutton his shirt in the hall. In the space of a minute the floor was littered with items of clothing. At this juncture the door opened again, and his wife walked in.

'Oh, mm, Andrea,' Michael took refuge in politeness, 'this is—'

'I know who this is,' said Andrea, squeezing past them. 'Nice tattoos, Miss Jones!' She disappeared upstairs. They hurriedly dressed and retired to the lounge where a bottle of wine was breathing. Michael poured them a glass each and they sat at either end of the three-seater sofa, sipping innocently.

'I like your curtains,' Amelanchier said.

* * *

There was much activity in the Council's offices over the following two days. As demanded by the chief executive, each of his chief officers had come up with proposals for savings to be made in each of their departments, savings which were quantified by their colleagues and formulated into the report which Jenkins presented to a rapidly convened full Council meeting. The cleaners had hardly restored the Council Chamber to a presentable state following the meeting which had thrown out Groat's housing scheme. Several agendas from that evening remained on seats to confuse the less astute members, who weren't quite sure why they were there. They soon found out.

At the end of the week the *Glostwich Bugle* carried a banner headline.

FIASCO AT THE COUNCIL
Chief Executive Suspended as Civic Centre Axed

Work on the new civic centre at Fairybridge Court has been halted, probably permanently, following the discovery of a major miscalculation of resources in the treasurer's department of Glostover District Council, which has left the project severely underfunded. The treasurer, George O'Rourke, has accepted responsibility and resigned. But councillors have also suspended Hywel Jenkins, who as chief executive was in overall command. The Council's solicitor will assume overall control on a temporary basis.

Mr Jim Randall, of local builders, Vogue and Randall, the contractors on the grandiose Fairybridge project, said 'It's a complete cock-up, they couldn't organise a p— up in a brewery. We will be claiming compensation in the courts.' The basement of the civic centre, which was to provide free parking for the Council's staff, is virtually complete.

A photograph of the basement occupied half of the front page. Several bricklayers stood around morosely, trowels in hand. Mick Mulvey, the site agent, in his blue safety helmet, stared at the camera in the foreground and pointed at something to his right as requested by the *Bugle*'s photographer.

The report continued on the inside pages:

> The deputy treasurer, Kevin Cash, has replaced his former boss, with his own post abolished to reduce the salary bill. Further savings have included the early retirement of the chief technical services officer with immediate effect and the amalgamation of most of his department with Housing, to form a new department of Housing and Environmental Services. The exception is the Architects' Section which has been disbanded, and Maxwell Spynk and his team made redundant. The one female architect, mother-of-two Julia Faraday, 34, has joined the Planning Department as architectural adviser.

Julia was the only officer to merit a photograph. The new treasurer would have readily conceded his legs were not in the same league as hers. Many of the *Bugle*'s male readers found their attention wandering at that point in the report, and consequently missed the less remarkable news that Glostwich Library was to close at the end of the financial year, and that the gypsy sites, to which the *Bugle* had led popular opposition, were to be abandoned. The public toilets, however, had narrowly escaped closure.

Someone at the Council meeting had raised the same question for which the chief planner had previously been ridiculed. Could the former owner be persuaded to take the land back and refund the purchase price? Marcus Groat was absent from the meeting, having succumbed to a nervous complaint following the rejection of his housing proposal. Knowing Groat's character, it was felt by the members that a refund was a long shot. The acting chief executive was, nevertheless, instructed to pursue the matter. Robert Snow could sense that there was a further political opportunity here. The time had come to make his move.

Chapter Eighteen

Marcus Groat opened the letter which had just been delivered through his front door and walked reading it into the drawing room of Groat Hall. The letter was on the headed notepaper of Glostover District Council and signed by the acting chief executive. It explained the Council's present financial difficulties and very politely asked Marcus if he would consider refunding the purchase price of the land at Fairybridge and taking it back into his estate.

He laughed. It was not a pleasant laugh; some would describe it as vindictive. Virginia looked up enquiringly from the jigsaw she was doing.

'They have a nerve, some people,' said Marcus, 'think that I'm going to cough up the money they paid me for the civic centre site, with a generous discount I might add, just because somebody made an almighty cock-up. No, that money's staying where it is in the Cayman Islands!'

'Where are they, the Cayman Islands?'

'God knows, somewhere in mid Atlantic, I think. Doesn't really matter.'

'It might, if we needed it in a hurry.' Her husband smiled indulgently.

'It's not like drawing some cash out from your Post Office account,' he said, 'my accountant knows exactly how much I have and where it is.'

'Isn't it my money actually?' Virginia asked innocently. Groat glanced sharply at his wife. His smile had disappeared.

'Well, technically it is, but only for tax purposes. What's yours is ours, and you don't have to worry your head about financial affairs.'

'Only, the ruin you sold was my family's home, and the land where you were going to build a housing scheme was part of the estate.' She shuffled the jigsaw pieces around the box, looking for a blue bit with some white on the edge. Groat felt uneasy. He looked down at his wife. Surely it wasn't Virginia who had got the Americans involved. They were on the same side, were they not? And Virginia didn't have the nous to do something like that off her own bat. Did she?

Groat retired to his study and dashed off a reply to the acting chief executive. Being somewhat rattled, he was not as diplomatic as he probably should have been. The following day the letter was leaked to the press and was shortly afterwards quoted verbatim on the front page of the *Bugle*. The headline read:

COUNCIL FUNDS SECRETED OFFSHORE
Chairman refuses to reimburse public money
paid for civic centre site.

Following the recent débâcle at Glostover District Council, it has emerged that its chairman, Councillor Marcus Groat, sold the land, formerly belonging to his wife's family, to the Council and is now refusing to bail out the beleaguered bureaucrats by reversing the transaction. A considerable number of staff have lost their jobs, and the site is blighted by the construction of the basement now, like the staff, redundant. There have been calls for the politicians to take their share of the blame.

The road, which was to have served the doomed civic centre, would also have been essential to give access to Marcus Groat's proposed housing estate which was recently rejected by Planning Committee. The access only became possible following an unfortunate accident which destroyed the derelict chapel of Fairybridge Court, due to be restored as the new Council Chamber. The chapel was believed to be the work of the late Victorian architect, C. P. Hopwood.

There was further criticism; enough to justify Robert Snow's call for an extraordinary Council meeting, the second that month. There was just one item on the agenda, a vote of confidence in the council's chairman, which Groat lost by a large margin. He had no choice but to resign. Then someone nominated Robert Snow to replace him, and Snow was dragged metaphorically to the rostrum like a speaker of the House of Commons. A new era had begun in Glostover District Council.

* * *

Michael's search for a new job was not going well. Until the divorce settlement was determined he was stuck with the house and continuing to pay the mortgage, so that any job had to be within commuting distance of Glostwich. The dissolution of the Architects' Section had released competitors into the job market, and private practices were often reluctant to take on in-house employees, whom they considered unlikely to have the right work ethic. He was sleeping badly.

After a couple of pints in the Jolly Huntsman one evening, he retired to bed early with the latest edition of *The Architects'*

Journal, at the back of which various posts were advertised. There was one in the Birmingham office of the Midland Bank, just about commutable, and with the sort of salary and perks you would expect from a bank. He resolved to apply the following day, flipping through the pages to an article about the architecture of Pompeii, which he and Andrea had visited while holidaying in nearby Sorrento. Pompeii was not Andrea's scene, though she had liked the explicit murals. What had impressed Michael was the way the wealthier Romans had created private but well-lit and ventilated homes in the centre of a tumultuous city, presenting a blank wall to the street broken only by a single entrance door, then wrapping the rooms around a central atrium open to the sky. He pulled the duvet higher and tried to concentrate on the article and its photographs. There was much to take in, many discoveries having been made since their visit.

It was not long, however, before his eyelids drooped, and the magazine slipped out of his hand onto the bedroom floor. He wrapped his toga more tightly around himself. You'd have thought a Roman town house on the Bay of Naples would be warmer than this. Across the room, Andrea lay on a marble slab, ensconced in cushions, while Oliver in a ludicrously short tunic fed her grapes. Seeing him stir, a slave girl topped up Michael's goblet with red wine from a pitcher. Across her naked back was tattooed the legend, *Gladiators Rule OK*. Would there be anything else, master? He waved her away.

In the atrium he could see a distinguished looking man with a crown of laurel leaves holding forth to a bunch of sycophants. He was patently Charles Pericles Hopwood, but all addressed him as Caesar. Michael rose and wandered out to see what was going on.

'Yea, I got as far as the Rubicon,' Caesar was boasting, 'and I thought to hell with it.' He proceeded to bad-mouth his enemies, Pompey and crew, at the same time extolling his own achievements.

'I came, I saw, I—'

'Conned the lot of us,' someone said, and the mood of the crowd changed. Several of them produced short swords from their togas and advanced on Caesar. 'Take that,' snarled the instigator, plunging his sword into Caesar's body, the rest following suit. C.P. fell against the water feature as Michael drew a weapon from under his toga and moved forward.

'Et tu, Michael!' The pool turned red. Then there was a loud rumble which grew to a great crash and the sky went dark. People were running, women screaming. He dashed out into the street to see Vesuvius spewing out its contents, a huge black cloud rolling down the mountain side towards the town. Ahead of it a stream of humanity, the odd chariot, mostly on foot, all terrified. He ran back into the house, but Andrea had disappeared. The slave girl was cowering in a corner. He grabbed her hand and made for the door, where someone resembling Kirk Douglas in a loin cloth, slung her over his shoulder and made off down the street.

'Oh, Spartacus,' she cried, 'I knew you'd come!'

'There's gratitude,' Michael thought, as six soldiers yomped past him.

'Don't hang about, buddy,' one of them said through the gum he was chewing, 'get the hell outta here!' Then a wall collapsed on them. He started to run, tripped over his toga, and fell flat on his face. At this point he awoke, tangled in his duvet on the bedroom floor. He lay there for some time, sweating. He'd thought there was something dodgy about his second pint in the Huntsman.

* * *

The decree nisi came through Michael's letterbox the following morning. After the volcanic eruption of his dream, it was a damp squib. Their solicitors had advised he and Andrea not to go down the adultery road, both being guilty, though Michael argued he would not have been, had Andrea not strayed first. It had been agreed that once the decree had become Absolute, the house would be sold, the mortgage paid off and whatever money and goods remained would be equally shared between them. He rang Jane to tell her the news. They talked on the phone for the best part of an hour, neither voicing their ache to meet, frustrated by the necessity to maintain uninvolved until all was settled.

There were no such complications with Amelanchier, however. He took her for a celebratory drink, then a walk through the grounds of Fairybridge, to see how the newts were getting on. They were in fact breeding. The site of the abandoned civic centre was sad and silent, as places where once men worked tend to be. Rogue and Vandal had removed their huts, their plant and loose materials, their security fencing and signs. Michael and Amelanchier stood on the rim and looked down. To most people it was just an extensive concrete slab with blockwork walls around its perimeter rising to ground level. But Michael saw beyond the surface. He knew that the floor slab was a raft, heavily reinforced with steel, with a waterproof bituminous membrane sandwiched inside it, that the membrane was continued within the blockwork walls, so that ground water could not penetrate, even under pressure. What a waste! As they walked away through the woods, Michael was thoughtful. An idea was forming in his head. It was soon to vanish.

'I've been meaning to tell you,' Amelanchier said, hesitantly, 'Laurence is going out to Nicaragua, to help the locals to build a couple of schools in remote settlements.'

'Good for him,' Michael said, 'sounds like a worthwhile project.'

'And he's asked me to go with him.' She stopped and looked at him. 'I said yes.'

Michael was taken aback. 'How long will you be away?'

'About a year, maybe fifteen months.' She pulled herself against him. 'It's something I need to do, for humanity. It's like I've been called.' Michael held her closely. Her cheek was surprisingly damp against his. Although the news had come as a shock, he knew it was inevitable. You couldn't keep a butterfly in a jar.

'If that's how it is, you must do it,' he told her, 'I'll probably still be around when you get back.' She shook her head.

'No, that wouldn't be fair on you, Michael. And besides, Laurence and I are sort of—'

Ah, Michael thought, there was something of Spartacus about Laurence. But he kissed her anyway. There were lots of nasty things that could happen to a gladiator in the jungles of Nicaragua. Unfortunately, they could happen to slave girls too.

* * *

Marcus Groat was not feeling well. Since he'd been deposed as chairman of the Council, he had lost his appetite, formerly voracious, had lots of headaches and been constantly fatigued. The world had turned against him. He had turned against the world. Waking in his bedroom from an afternoon sleep, he slouched across the carpet to the window, and drew back the curtains. The large garden, with sweeping lawns and colourful beds, with adolescent trees and shrubberies of contrasting foliage, would at one time have reassured him of his prestige, his place in the scheme of things. He would have felt socially superior to the gardener, hoeing and snipping in a distant corner. But not today.

He heard below him the front door opening, voices, the door closing and feet crunching the gravel, before the owner of the feet came into his field of vision. Then he gasped. It was that young architect whom he believed had scotched his plans, who had become the focus of his resentment, his hatred even. The architect, Maby was his name, got into the modest car that Groat had assumed belonged to the gardener, and drove off. Groat stumbled down the stairs, leaning heavily on the handrail and burst into the drawing room, where Virginia was moving about something metallic in a cardboard box.

'What,' he croaked, 'was that fellow doing in my house, chatting up my wife, after all the grief he has caused me?' Virginia met his glare.

'Mr Maby,' she said, 'was not chatting up your wife, as you crudely put it. He brought me these rosettes which were part of the staircase in my family home, in Fairybridge Court. He is a kind and considerate young man, and I will speak to whom I like inside or outside our house, Marcus Groat!'

Groat grabbed one of the rosettes from the box and threw it as hard as he could across the room. It smashed through a glass cabinet door and shattered several Royal Worcester plates within.

'That for your bloody family home,' he roared, 'I won't have it, I tell you. I won't—!'

Suddenly, his face took on a look of surprise. For a moment he stood erect, then he crumpled to the floor. Saliva ran from the corner of his mouth, he shuddered and laid still.

Virginia went quietly into the kitchen and reappeared with a dustpan and brush. She swept up the broken glass and porcelain and took it out to the dustbin. Then she rang 999.

* * *

When Michael got home from Groat Hall, his phone was ringing too. It was the matron of Wyebrae Nursing Home. She had been on the point of leaving him a message.

'It's Mrs Hopwood-Brown,' she told him, 'she's not very well and it appears she has no close relatives. Outlived them all. The only visitors she's had for some time are you and her solicitor in Shrewsbury. I just thought it would be comforting if you came to see her, Mr Maby. I appreciate you're a busy man and would quite understand if you can't make it.'

If only, thought Michael. He glanced at his watch.

'I'll be over within the hour, matron. You can tell her I'm on my way.'

Chapter Nineteen

Dora had certainly deteriorated. She was lying in bed with her upper body and head propped up on pillows at forty-five degrees. Her face was ashen though someone had gone to some trouble to tidy her rebellious white hair. She smiled as Michael was shown into the room and extended a limp hand towards his. He pulled a chair to her bedside and sat, still holding her hand.

'How are you feeling, Mrs Hop—'

'Dora,' she corrected him, her voice quieter but still firm, 'I'm as well as can be expected. All things must end. But what about you, Michael? What about your wife, or is she your ex-wife now?' He told her about the decree nisi. 'And is there someone else in your life?'

'I have been seeing someone.' She studied his face.

'But not the right someone, I would say. She'll come, Michael, she'll come. Just don't look too hard, that's the answer. And what of your career?' He'd just posted an application to the Bank and told her so.

'Sounds pretty boring to me,' she said, 'I'm sure you could find something more exciting than that. You'll forgive an old lady lecturing you, but you should forget all this Arts and Crafts nostalgia and think modern. We've had two World Wars and a Depression since my father's heyday and we, or you rather, are heading for the new millennium!' She noticed his shoulders drooping and her voice softened.

'And talking about my father, how's the biography going?'

'Pretty well,' he lied, 'you'll be able to read the draft soon.'

'I don't think so, Michael,' she said, 'I won't be around for long, I'm afraid.' She dismissed his protests. 'But I've been thinking while lying here, there's nothing else to do, and I've remembered something about my father you may find interesting. You know he was a Pargetter?'

'You did mention it once, and your mother's diary seems to confirm it.'

'Yes, in fact he was the grand wizard, or whatever, of some kiln, I think that's what they called it, in Hampshire. I've never been a great fan of the Pargetters – seems to me they're a bunch of scoundrels. If your face didn't fit you were blackballed, which is what happened to a Captain Hodge – something, down there. But he didn't take it lying down and accused my father of hypocrisy. There was quite a scandal about it in the local press. I remember because there were family arguments. Aunt Isabel was involved.'

Captain, Hampshire? Michael thought, Captain Dodgson, he would bet, James Cranham's commanding officer at Mafeking. He kept it to himself, as Dora moved onto other things.

'So, what do you think of England's selection for the Test Series?' He mentioned several names he had heard on the radio. 'Oh no, not Emburey, he's right off form.' He let her talk, not knowing enough about cricket to venture an opinion. Then halfway through her discourse on whether a spin bowler should be included in the team, her eyelids drooped, and she fell asleep. He waited a while then let go of her hand.

He stopped at the office on his way out.

'Mrs Hopwood-Brown tires very quickly,' the matron told him, 'the doctor thinks she's failing but I'm sure your visit will have comforted her. Mr Drew has just rung to say he will call to see her tomorrow. Some people ask to see a priest. Not Dora, she wants a solicitor.' She smiled. 'Thank you for coming, Mr Maby. It was very kind of you.'

* * *

At home, Michael brought his old drawing board and frame from the garage and set it up in the lounge. There was no Andrea to complain any more. He found his tee-square in the loft, took from his brief case the drawing instruments, set-square, rapidograph and clutch pencil he had brought home from work. He put the rapidograph nibs in a solvent to dissolve the dried-up ink. They hadn't been used for a while. Then he brought a stool in from the breakfast bar in the kitchen, sat on it and stared at the blank A1 sheet of paper he had stuck to the drawing board with masking tape.

What had Dora said about modern, getting up to date? He thought about school of architecture, how he and his fellow students were encouraged to approach a design with an open mind, starting with a plan which answered the client's brief and made the best possible use of the site given them. The architecture would evolve later. Form followed function. This was not the approach he had taken with the civic centre; he'd been obsessed with Hopwood and the end of the nineteenth century, the plan compromised for an historic style. Maybe old Spynk had been right.

Okay, so how would he deal with the Fairybridge site in its present state, a big hole in the ground in an otherwise idyllic rural setting? He needed a theoretical project – the sort that the college lecturers would have come up with, something like a school or a library. What about, he thought with a sudden burst of inspiration, an art gallery? Why not!

He'd smuggled a set of prints out of the office a while before his forced departure, so he had an accurate to-scale plan of the basement to start from. He unrolled the plan and stuck it to his drawing with masking tape. Then he took a sheet of tracing paper, also purloined, laid it over the print, and with soft lead in his clutch pencil, began a freehand plan of an art gallery for the people of Glostwich, whether they deserved it or not.

The design evolved surprisingly quickly. Being underground, the perimeter blank wall had no windows in it so that the whole surface was available for the display of artwork. Like the Roman house in his dream, the gallery could receive natural light by being wrapped around a central atrium, open to the sky. The atrium wall would be all glass, allowing visitors to progress around the edge of the exhibition spaces, choosing to dally or move on as they wished. And all the time with a clear view into the atrium, or courtyard, which could be landscaped with planting, sculpture and water features. There would be sitting areas where visitors could relax with drinks and snacks from an onsite bar and kitchen.

And what of the roof of a single storey building which was below natural ground level? It was simple. Take the turf over it as far as the atrium. Then the gallery would have a minimal impact on the countryside, from most viewpoints you would hardly know it was there.

After a couple of hours, Michael sat back on his stool, feeling as he used to feel when he'd cracked a college scheme as a student. It was good, Dora had been right. It was time he brought himself back to the future. Just a pity that the gallery was a pipe dream, he would have liked to have seen it built. He went through to the kitchen to make himself a coffee. The kettle had just boiled when the doorbell rang. It was Amelanchier.

'We've got a flight from Heathrow on Friday,' she told him. 'I couldn't go without saying goodbye.' He invited her in. 'It's a long journey, we have to go via Miami.' He left her in the lounge and went back into the kitchen to make the extra coffee. When he returned, he found her leaning over his drawing board.

'Is this Fairybridge?' He sheepishly admitted it was. 'But it's brilliant, Michael, it virtually returns the site to nature. Does it have to be about art, or could it be a museum of biodiversity, perhaps?'

'Well, yes,' he said. 'It could be all sorts of things, but it's just an exercise. There's no chance of actually building it.'

'Well, there should be, what's to stop you?' Michael smiled ruefully.

'There's the small question of money. And ownership.' Practicalities like that were not high on Amelanchier's priority list. 'But enough of me. What about you two and Nicaragua?'

'We two? I'm not the only one going with Laurence.' She mentioned three more names, all of them female. It sounded like a great arrangement, Michael thought.

'It's just that I thought you and Laurence were—'

'Oh, don't be so old fashioned, Michael. It's not an exclusive relationship. For instance, it doesn't stop me staying the night here.'

'Really?'

'Really,' she said, stroking the back of his neck, 'but only if you run me home in the morning.' He switched off his angle-poise lamp.

'Now where did we get to,' said Amelanchier, 'with those lessons in botany?'

* * *

The day that Laurence and his entourage took off for Miami, Michael received another call from the matron at Wyebrae. She was sorry to have to tell him that Mrs Hopwood-Brown had passed away during the previous afternoon. Michael felt empty, though he had expected the news.

'Did she suffer, Matron?' he asked.

'Not at all. She was as lucid as ever. Her last request was to know the latest score at Headingley. When we told her she just closed her eyes and went to sleep. And that was that.'

The funeral was to be held at Hereford Crematorium, Tuesday week. He thanked the matron for informing him and put the phone down. Another departure. The train had left the station, the platform was empty. He wondered what the future had in store.

* * *

Virginia closed the door behind the last guest and heaved a sigh of relief. Her husband's funeral had been a strain, not so much from grief as from keeping up the appearance of grief. The church had been bursting with mourners, chiefly Pargetters, as was the norm when one of their brethren turned up his toes. Most of the Glostover District councillors also put in an appearance, including the new chairman, Robert Snow. It wouldn't do to be anything but magnanimous with the press and public present. The singing of hymns had been enthusiastic, far surpassing the murmured contributions of the usual funeral service. For once, the voice of the vicar was lost. And after the funeral a few friends, they were indeed few, and family, mostly distant, had assembled at Groat Hall for refreshments, prepared by local caterers, Gourmets de Glostwich and served on Virginia's china plates.

The conversation had been light and inconsequential. There was no mention of the deceased. The gardens of the hall were admired, as were its spacious rooms. Several people questioned the missing cabinet door, which Virginia explained was being restored by an expert cabinet maker following an unfortunate accident with a tea trolley. The guests nibbled their canapés and sipped their low-alcohol Chardonnays, then one by one took their leave, their car tyres churning up the carefully raked gravel in front of the house. Now at last Virginia was alone.

She discarded the black crêpe shawl she had worn around her shoulders all day and kicked off her heeled black shoes. Her soft grey dress was subdued but not sombre. She felt she could happily wear it for future, less solemn occasions. She could wear whatever she liked, now Marcus had gone. It was all going to be different. He had treated the assets she had brought to the marriage with impunity, as if they were his own. Now she was in control of her family legacy, with the bonus of the Groat fortune too.

She looked around the room. It was dark, tired and boring. It needed less furniture, lighter colours, fresh fabrics. Still sophisticated, respectful of its heritage, of course, Waring and Gillow, paints by Farrow and Ball, to her taste, no one else's. She had always held sway in the garden, Marcus being uninterested in horticulture, and had developed over the years a feeling for landscape. It was in her blood. But now she wanted a bigger canvas, a background to her family portraits, a canvas she could restore to its former glory. Her husband had refused out of spite to cooperate with the Council, but he was gone. She resolved to reverse his decision, and to take Fairybridge back under her wing. She munched a canapé and poured herself a large glass of wine, fully alcoholic. Life promised a great deal.

* * *

The funeral service for Dora Hopwood-Brown could hardly have been more different to that of Marcus Groat. Apart from the professional celebrant, there were just four mourners at the crematorium – Michael, her solicitor, Mr Drew, and the matron and another nurse from Wyebrae. There were no relatives or old friends, Dora having outlived them all.

The celebrant did her best with the rudimentary information the carers had been able to give her. They knew that Dora was the daughter of a famous architect and an architect herself, that she was a widow twice over but had no children, and that she was an ardent cricket fan. 'And tennis player,' Mr Drew whispered in Michael's ear.

The curtain closed in front of the coffin to the music Dora had chosen, defiant to the last, the choral movement from Beethoven's Ninth, the *Ode to Joy*. Michael walked slowly back to the carpark with Mr Drew. The old solicitor was quiet, there was a catch in his voice.

'I came to see Mrs Hopwood-Brown the other day at her request. She has left twenty-five per cent of her estate to the Lords Taverners. You may know that they are a charity who support cricket, particularly disadvantaged and disabled young players.' Michael murmured his approval. It was what he would have expected from the old lady. Mr Drew stopped and turned to face him.

'The remaining seventy-five per cent, Mr Maby, she has left to you. It is a substantial amount. You are a very fortunate young man, Michael, very fortunate indeed!' Michael was dumbstruck.

'But what, why – she hardly knew me,' he stammered.

'From what she told me, she was touched by your kindness, and felt you needed a break. I have been her solicitor for many years, and I know she was an excellent judge of character.'

Michael sat heavily on a seat alongside the path.

'She also said that you were in the process of a divorce. So, with your approval, I can delay the settlement of the will until after your decree absolute. We don't want your soon to be ex-wife to take a share, do we?'

'I suppose not,' said Michael. There was too much to take in already.

'Well, it will be a little while before the estate is determined, but I can tell you the approximate sum.' He stooped to whisper a figure in Michael's ear as some late mourners for the next service hurried past. 'I will write to confirm the details. In the meantime, I offer you my congratulations, Mr Maby.' Michael shook his proffered hand and watched him shuffle off towards his car. 'Goodbye for now,' he called over his shoulder.

Michael remained seated. He tilted his head back and watched the white clouds floating beneath what he now recognised as a blue summer sky. A distant plane drew its vapour trail across his whole field of vision.

'Thank you, Dora,' he addressed the heavens, 'thank you very, very much!' He was still sitting there when the mourners from the next service departed. They eyed him curiously.

Chapter Twenty

Taking the country way home from Dora's funeral, Michael drove past the entrance to Fairybridge Court, where he was surprised to see Virginia Groat pressed against the gate and gazing intently into the grounds. He pulled in behind her car and got out.

'Michael!' she greeted him. 'How nice to see you.' She was wearing a knee-length sage green dress and a darker green gilet, casual but elegant. She also looked, Michael thought, younger.

'I was sorry to hear of your loss,' he said. She nodded perfunctorily.

'But we must move on, Michael. I was standing here thinking about how we could turn the recent farce into something positive. I know we can never return to the golden days of my family's past, and I'm not sure it would be desirable anyway. It was a very privileged life. I would very much like to create something here at Fairybridge for the benefit of all, a country park perhaps, a nature reserve. The professor at the planning meeting was very enthusiastic about our wildflowers, I understand. Said it should be a Site of Special Scientific Interest, at least.' Michael looked away. 'And then there's those poor American soldiers. I'd like to set aside an area for them. Except we don't know the exact location of their graves.'

'There's something called GPR,' Michael said, 'that lets archaeologists find things underground without digging. You could try that.'

'Now that would be wonderful.' Virginia looked thoughtful.
'You know,' she said eventually, 'I was very conscious during my
husband's funeral, that the church service was over the top. He
wasn't religious, and neither am I. When it comes to it, I would
like to go quietly, and have my ashes buried under a tree where
friends could come and remember me. There are many people
I think, who would feel the same. Why not give them such a
place at Fairybridge? They could purchase plots for themselves
in advance, alongside the Americans. And choose an appropriate
tree.'

'It wouldn't even be a change of use,' Michael said. Then,
'Sorry, I didn't mean to be flippant. It comes of working with
planners.' Virginia, however, smiled. 'It's a great idea,' he said
gently, 'but you don't own all the land anymore, do you? The
land on which the court stood now belongs to Glostover District
Council, and they wouldn't have the resources to invest in the
sort of scheme you're suggesting, even if they wanted to!'

'True. But the Council offered to sell it back to my late
husband, who turned them down. Now I make the decisions,
and I want to accept the offer.'

'It then becomes a private initiative.' Michael nodded slowly.
'If you're sure about that, Mrs Groat. But can I suggest you
don't sound too eager. Let then think you're doing them a favour.
They've managed to make some savings, but they still need to
recoup the major cost of the land. You'll be getting them out of
a large hole.' He grinned. 'Literally!'

'I'm glad you can laugh about things,' Virginia said, 'it can't
have been easy for you. Have you managed to find a job yet?'
He told her about the bank. 'Just that I have been thinking
about converting the stables at Groat Hall into holiday lets, and

wondered if you would be interested in designing them for me?'
He arranged to do a survey at the end of the week. He could
have done it the following day but didn't want to seem too eager.

* * *

Instead, Michael occupied the following day with clearing his
house of unwanted stuff. One pile for recycling, another for the
charity shops, a third for Andrea's belongings, the latter filling the
spare bedroom. His head was buzzing with ideas. Dora's legacy
was life changing. It meant he could set up his own practice,
with funds behind him to bridge the initial period. He could
keep the house for a time after the divorce, just as a base while
he built his dream house, no longer Hopwoodesque and not,
sadly, involving green wellies and a golden-haired child on his
shoulders. The spaniel of his dream remained.

He emptied drawers with abandon, discarding shoes and
stuffing black bin-liners with shirts and sweaters, cardboard boxes
with magazines and dog-eared paperbacks. Attacking a pile of
Andrea's pot boilers, he came across a stranger, British Birds and
Their Haunts. Andrea and ornithology didn't mix. He opened
the book to discover Jane's name on the title page, her maiden
name, written in a careful adolescent hand. She must have left
the book on a previous visit. He ran his finger over the letters.

That evening he drove over to Church Newington, the bird book
and a bottle of Sauvignon blanc on the passenger seat. If he had
been expecting a sophisticated woman in a red dress, or possibly
tennis shorts, he would have been disappointed. Jane answered the
doorbell in a comfortable old sweater and jeans. She was patently
disconcerted by his visit, reluctant to invite him in. When he did

make it over the threshold, she regaled him with apologies, the state of the lounge, the unwashed pots, the drooping house plants.

'You ought to see my place,' he said.

'But you're a bloke, it's expected. And look at my hair,' she said despairingly, brushing the said locks away from her face. 'I'm just not ready for visitors.'

'Hey! Remember me? I'm Michael, old friend and admirer. And your hair looks fine to me, Jane, as does the rest of you.' She half smiled, then burst into tears. And suddenly she was in his arms, sobbing against his shoulder.

'Sorry, Michael. It's been hard, the last few months! It must have been the same for you.' He nodded.

'It's nearly over.' He was about to say what a bastard Oliver was but thought better of it. He wasn't sure how she felt about her soon to be ex-husband. Instead, he held her tightly until the sobs subsided.

'I can't offer you anything to go with the wine,' she said eventually, 'there's nothing in the fridge.'

'Look, why don't I go and get a takeaway,' Michael said, 'and give you a chance to wash your hair, paint your nails, and completely spring clean the whole house while I'm away?' Jane laughed between the sniffs.

'That would be good. Nothing too spicy though, chicken fried rice maybe.' He opened the front door. 'I think I could find a couple of yoghurts for afters,' she said, 'black cherry alright?'

Michael strolled the short distance into the town. There were several people waiting for their orders outside the Chinese takeaway.

'Ready in twenty minutes,' said the cheerful proprietor, as he added Michael's order to the list. 'That alright, sir?'

Michael crossed the road and found a seat on the bank of the river which bisected the town. The longer wait the better he thought. He hadn't really appreciated Jane's losses before, her husband, her best friend and her self-confidence. He'd only lost a wife, and there were compensations a' plenty for the loss of his job, foremost, of course, Dora's legacy. He had resolved, with some degree of guilt, to avoid disclosing that to Jane at present, not wishing it to be a factor in their relationship. He closed his eyes and let the sounds of the shallows wash over him, only realising he'd fallen asleep when someone opened the takeaway door and yelled out his number.

Jane had taken full advantage of his absence. The house appeared immaculate, though Michael was aware of the landslide of belongings which would probably issue from the cupboards should someone inadvertently open them. Jane herself was a vision, a dress, not however, red, had replaced the jeans and sweater. Her hair was washed and brushed, and an aura of freshness surrounded her. How, he wondered, did women manage to do that? She had even warmed the plates and put the wine in the fridge. He allowed himself one glass to her two, as they quietly disposed of the surprisingly tasty, if not exactly piping hot, takeaway.

'So, what are you hoping to do?' Michael asked as he pushed his empty plate away. Jane finished her last mouthful.

'Well, I've registered as a supply teacher. The work's erratic, but when there is a vacancy the money's good. I'll be buying Oliver out, but he's been adjudged to own just twenty-five per cent of the house.'

'Will you be okay financially?'

'It'll be hard, but I'll manage,' Jane said firmly, 'what about you? Any sign of a new job?'

'I'm going out on my own,' Michael said, 'got my first commission already.' Jane raised her eyebrows.

'Just like Oliver was always pushing you to do.' She was quiet for a moment. 'Bastard!'

'Andrea too,' Michael countered. 'Bitch!' They frowned at each other, then their expressions cracked and together they burst into uncontrollable laughter. It was sometime before he was able to top up her glass without shaking. She nodded through her tears towards his glass.

'Driving!' Michael said, shaking his head. Jane looked at him coyly.

'You don't have to drive.' He hesitated, then filled his glass too. 'Only this time,' she said, 'don't spend the whole night in the bathroom.'

* * *

At the end of the week, as promised, Michael turned up at Groat Hall with a fifteen-metre tape, a pencil and survey pad. Virginia showed him the stable block and left him to it. It was a long single storey building with a Welsh slate roof, sub-divided by brick walls into five luxurious equine apartments. It had been some time since it was occupied. The survey took little more than an hour. He took some photographs and was loading the boot when Virginia appeared at the front door and called him in for a coffee.

'So, what do you think?

'I would say that the individual stables are too small for anything but single lets,' Michael said, sipping his milky brew, 'and those aren't very lettable. What I suggest is that we make the two end stables into double bedrooms with en-suites, each linked to a living room and kitchenette in the adjoining stable. The middle stable could be another double bedroom with doors into both apartments, so that it could be let with either to accommodate a family or two couples.' Virginia was delighted.

'That would be perfect, Michael! Just the sort of thing I had vaguely in mind for so long, and you've put it into focus. Can't wait to see the drawings! Things are certainly going to change around here, here and at Fairybridge.'

'And have you made any progress there, Mrs Groat?'

'Virginia, please!' said Virginia. 'Well, I've been talking to the Nature Conservatory about restoring the parkland, species of trees and so on. And dredging the lake without harming the newts. The thing that worries me most is the great hole in the middle where the new offices were going to be. It will take a fortune to fill it, and years for it to recover.' Michael took a deep breath and looked at her full in the face.

'You don't need to fill it, Virginia. Turn it into an asset.' She stared.

'What do you mean?'

'What you have there is an excellent base for a building, with external walls up to ground level, all waterproofed. Make it into a visitors' centre for your park. Put on a flat roof and extend the surrounding grassland over it. You'd hardly know it was there.' Virginia looked doubtful.

'But wouldn't it be dark and dismal?' Michael shook his head.

'No. In the centre we would have a large courtyard, open to the sky and surrounded by a glass wall with planting, seats and sculpture. Visitors could circulate behind the glass, under cover, while further back and out of direct sunlight would be exhibition spaces where you could display all manner of things – local art, archaeology, natural history. It's up to you.'

Virginia's face was a picture. He watched as his words sunk in.

'It's a wonderful idea, Michael,' she said eventually, 'but I'm not sure I could afford it, after buying back the land and everything.'

'Well, for a start, you'd be saving the cost of filling the hole, which would be substantial. Then this is very much the type of project that the National Lottery likes to support. We might be able to get something from the County Council on a match funding basis, or even from Glostover D.C. You would after all, be attracting visitors from a wide area and there are lots of councillors with cafés and shops. Or holiday lets to fill,' he added.

'I like it, I really do!' Virginia said. 'But will that be sufficient?'

'Probably not,' said Michael, 'and that's where I come in.' He took a deep breath. 'I've come into some money, quite a lot of money actually, and I want to invest some of it in a worthwhile project, like this.'

He had her attention.

'I've been doing some research recently and discovered that Fairybridge Court had a gatehouse at the point where the drive left the road, where we were talking the other day.'

'Yes,' she interrupted, 'just some low walls left, covered in ivy.'

'Well, if you were to sell it to me, together with a moderate piece of woodland, to build myself a house, you'd give yourself a cash injection. I am also willing to invest in the visitors' centre itself, and of course, to provide free architectural services for the project.' He sat back, dazed by his own audacity. Virginia was stunned.

'Heavens, Michael, you've sprung one on me there!' She studied the stern face of a Groat ancestor on the wall opposite. 'This is game changing. Are you suggesting we should form a partnership?'

'Yes, I think I am.' She shook her head in disbelief.

'That's an awful lot to take in. I would have to think very carefully about it, get some professional business advice, talk to my solicitor. I have to say, however, it does seem an attractive idea on the face of it. And it would be good to have a constant presence on site, even when the park and visitors' centre were closed to the public. Someone I could trust. I can't give you an answer now, but I will come back to you as soon as possible. Give me some time, will you?'

'Of course,' Michael said. It felt good, being an entrepreneur!

* * *

During the next few weeks, things moved rapidly. Virginia spoke to the acting chief executive at the district council and informed him that she had reconsidered her former husband's rejection of the Council's offer to sell Fairybridge to the Groats. She felt it was incumbent on her family, she said, to support the Council in its hour of need.

'Don't bite her hand off,' advised Chairman Robert Snow. But there had been no other offers and a contract was quickly drawn up in-house and signed by both parties. To offset the cost of restoring Fairybridge to parkland, a discount had been applied to the original sum which the Council had paid to her husband. Virginia was once again the owner of her family's estate. She had talked things over with professional advisers and was ready to form a partnership with Michael, assuming the visitors' centre was financially viable. And to this end he had worked up the drawings and arrived at an estimated cost with one of Glostover's redundant and consequently vengeful quantity surveyors. It all depended on planning permission now.

Having secured the land, the unlikely partnership of Groat and Maby went with a more detailed set of design drawings to see

Geoff Lomax at the planning department. Geoff was impressed, as was his architectural adviser whom he called in to the meeting. The restoration and enhancement of the parkland was about as contentious as apple pie and motherhood, the creation of a woodland cemetery also having the precedent of the American graves. Both officers liked the way the proposed new building made so little impact on the landscape, especially in contrast to its defunct predecessor.

Michael's house, though it was not referred to thus, was replacing a ruined gatehouse and still, in fact, acting as a control point for visitors, though they needed to see its detailed design. Of course, as officers, they couldn't say yea or nay, but Geoff anticipated that the whole project would find favour with the Council. A country park and visitors' centre would bring tourists into the town, and as Michael had said, many of the councillors were shopkeepers and restaurateurs. And then there was the increasingly important green vote.

'Nice job, Michael,' Julia said quietly as they were leaving, 'I knew there was a modernist in there somewhere, trying to get out.' He could have taken that as patronising, but he knew Julia only said what she meant. And she was right, he had changed.

He said goodbye to Virginia and took the stuff he'd sorted for recycling to the tip, then two supermarket bags of books to Oxfam. Among them, *C. P. Hopwood: The Middle Years.*

'That looks valuable,' the volunteer lady opined.

'Not to me,' said Michael, 'once it might have been!'

EPILOGUE

Two years have passed. The edges of woodland around Fairybridge Court have been enhanced with marginal planting, wild cherry and field maple, at strategic points new copses created of beeches, oaks and horse chestnuts. All these trees are in their second season of growth.

Experts with GPR have located the graves of the American soldiers and the site has become the centre of a woodland cemetery. A score of people have reserved plots and specified trees to mark them, the ashes of three clients already interred. A small summerhouse occupies the knoll on which Hopwood's chapel once stood, where relatives can sit quietly in sight of their loved ones. The United States government has authorised an annual grant for the upkeep of the area.

Part of the lake has been deepened, and some of the shallows cleared of choking vegetation, the newts being given a short vacation meantime. Rainwater from the visitors' centre tops up the lake, and the lake returns the favour by supplying the heat pump which keeps the visitors' centre warm.

To minimise the risk of trampling wildflowers, mown grass paths are maintained through the woods and meadows and visitors requested to stick to them. Included in the entrance fee, guides are available to help identify the plants and talk about biodiversity. One of these guides on certain days is a Miss A.

Jones, whose forename few can pronounce. Miss Jones has been sworn to secrecy on the origin of some of the rare plants and her former relationship with the custodian. She is popular with younger visitors on account of her tattoos and tales of the jungles of Central America.

Virginia Groat herself is often seen around the gallery and is more than happy to talk about the exhibits with visitors, particularly the section dealing with the history of Fairybridge Court and her family. She enthuses too about the gallery for local artists, and sculptures displayed in the courtyard, not a few of which have been sold to patrons from London and beyond. She is not so well informed about natural history but learning fast.

The custodian of the Dora Hopwood-Brown Gallery has little contact with the public but is a presence and can be glimpsed in his small office across the courtyard, working at his drawing board on one of several design projects coming his way as a result of the popularity of the gallery. He is having to turn jobs down. The gallery has been shortlisted for the RIBA Marches Region's building of the year. Fellow architects ignore the exhibits and take photographs of the building itself, among them Maxwell Spynk, who nods his approval to the angel above the Custodian's head.

To the three clients interred in the woodland cemetery, Michael has added the ashes of a fourth, his benefactor, Dora. And if her spirit was to wander the grounds after the visitors departed some fine evening, it would discover, tucked away by the woods, a cricket practice area with nets, another tribute to her generosity.

On such an evening, Michael puts the top on his rapidograph, switches off his angle poise lamp, and lets himself out of the deserted visitors' centre. At the top of the pedestrian ramp, he pauses to admire the sunset reflected in the lake before continuing along the drive into the birchwood. A woodpecker chuckles in the greenery, as his house comes into view. Cottage Orné would describe it best, the style advocated by the Planning Department as being most suitable for the replacement of an early nineteenth-century gatehouse. He has not disputed this, as it tells potential clients he can design in period styles as well as modern.

As he opens the front door, his springer spaniel, Mafeking (Maff for short) rushes to greet him. He fusses the dog and moves into the lounge where his wife is reading on the settee. He sits beside her, puts his right arm around her shoulders and places his left hand gently on her swollen belly.

'Is she alright?'

Jane snuggles against him. 'She's fine.'

The golden-haired boy of his former dreams has somehow morphed into a dark and beautiful girl like her mother.

'What would you like for supper?' he says. 'I'll make it!'

'I just fancy cauliflower cheese!' He looks at her, startled, but Jane is smiling. She knows the story. 'Which reminds me of something I heard today,' she says, 'evidently Oliver and your ex-wife were driving out in the country, probably too fast, when a child ran out into the road. Oliver braked and skidded into a gate post.'

'Oh, my God!' says Michael. 'Was anyone injured?'

'Evidently not, but the police got involved and Oliver had been drinking. He's in trouble!' Michael tries unsuccessfully not to smile.

'Where did you say it happened?'

'I didn't. It was that place you had a job a year or two back, near Drabley. Something Royal.'

'Princess Margaret Gardens,' he says.

About the Author

Martin Booth grew up in what was then a Yorkshire village and attended the grammar school in the nearby Lancashire town of Clitheroe. He trained as an architect in Liverpool where he met his wife who was from Worcestershire, and after qualifying moved to the Malvern area where they still live. Despite designing and building two houses for themselves in Malvern and in rural Herefordshire, he has still found time to write and to indulge his love of fell walking, particularly in the English Lake District. The couple have a daughter in Bath and a son and daughter-in-law and two granddaughters in Malvern. They themselves now live in the nearby village of Cradley.